Injustice Silence

by

Jax Delavega

ISBN:
eBook: 979-8-90224-100-3
Paperback: 979-8-90224-101-0
Hardback: 979-8-90224-102-7

Published by:
Authors Publishing House
178 Broadway, 3rd Floor, #1343
New York, NY 10001, USA

Main Line: (855) 624-0155
Email: support@authorspublishinghouse.com

Trigger Warning

"If you're going to read this, I can't help but let you know how deep we dive into trauma and things said in this book could cause triggers, we have two choices, hurt people hurt people or heal."

~ Author

Table of Contents

Dedication

To my children: You are the best version of me. Everything good that could be taken from me was multiplied threefold in you all. I love you more than words could ever express.

To my soul sisters, Coco and Marie: You loved me when I didn't love myself. Thank you for everything, there are not enough words to describe your beautiful, amazing, perfect faces and souls. I love that this will live forever in this book, just to make you cringe, my dear Coco.

To my sponsor, my Terri: I could not be living the life I have today without your guidance, sobriety experience, strength, and love. Thank you for being there for me throughout my sober journey and for reminding me that life is better sober, and that we can't just hang up on people when we don't like the truth and guidance they are giving us ;) I love you so much.

Evans Elementary: The staff, the teachers, Mrs. W, and Tate, you helped me raise these babies alone, with love, compassion, and full awareness of the darkness we were going through. You were there for me before sobriety and after, and you always treated me as a good mother regardless. You will never understand the depth of my love, or how a school could become family for me and my children. Thank you. They just don't make them like you all anymore.

Collin County DA: The team in March 2021. Thank you, for so many reasons. It's not easy, but you helped in every way to protect a child and do the right thing, legally and morally. You helped prepare me through so much hate and shame for doing the right thing, and you equipped me in the best possible way to take on something so difficult. You do this constantly. Thank you.

To my readers: Let's find justice. You can choose to be like those who hurt you, or you can choose to be better than them.

ii

Prologue

I was sitting there, trying to make sense of the situation. It felt like a nightmare, except you knew you were awake, with the confusion of how this could possibly be real. I felt numb and yet overwhelmed with sensation. It was like the feeling you get when you know something terrible has happened, but you cannot believe it and you do not want to. That was exactly how it felt, babbling, repetitive, pure insanity. I sat there listening to the news replay the story over and over, filled with many lies and many truths. It would not be the news without both. There was a ringing sound, and I was in a trance, wondering what was happening. Was that the TV? Was it in my head? I realized it was my doorbell. I got up off the floor, not realizing how long I had been sitting there, but long enough for it to hurt. As I walked over, I felt nervous about who might be at the door. My mother? No way. It had been over 24 hours since I made the call, and there had been no response, not a single word. Even when I told her what was happening, she acted as though she did not care, almost as if she wondered why I was even bothering her with this. I understood her reaction given the situation they were in, but it did nothing to help me process my feelings. I wondered who else might be questioning whether it was me, whether it was my last name they were hearing on the news, or whether they recognized his face and my connection to it.

I reached the door and opened it without thinking. All I saw were bright, flashing lights and microphones, with the same questions being shouted, the same ones over and over.

"Was it your daughter?" "Did you know?" "What happened here?" All reporters from different news stations, wanting more information than the small amount the Anna Police Department had decided to release to get their 15 minutes of fame. I truly do not blame them. I understand the desire to warn the public. I usually admire it and am thankful for the protection it offers my children and others, but today it was not protecting us. It was hurting us because of something horrendous someone else had done, my dad.

Chapter one

"Silence encourages the tormentor, never the tormented."

~ Elle Wiesel

I know the juiciness of the intro is what draws the eye or the reader, but that's not the sole purpose of the book, and yes, those play on words were intentional. There are so many layers to this book and this writing. We will come back to that eventually, but I want to share my experience and the many reasons I started writing this. This whole thing began with therapy, to put my feelings, my words, my shames, my situations, onto paper. There was nothing else that could fix my problems, and to this day, it might help you in some ways, and it might not. I can't predict your journey or your healing, but I reached a point where I was willing to try anything because nothing else was working. The constant drinking to avoid dealing with myself, the temporary numbing, the sweeping everything under the rug, the constant chaos of being a victim, strangely, just wasn't working. Huh, so weird. Isn't it crazy how exhausting being a victim can be? How can taking accountability feel like a fear? Facing reality can be sickening, and healing is the opposite of what that word seems to suggest. More like hurt.

For me, I was always the victim in many ways. Everything happened to me as an adult, and nothing was my fault. That alone was a hard pill to swallow, but what's inaccurate about the expression is how easy it was to literally swallow a pill or a drink rather than face the reality of my actions and the truth. I never realized that the shame that came from doing the right thing, or the shame of something happening to me or around me, contributed to my inability to live and my desire to numb something I couldn't understand or face.

This is not a book of bash or hate, and it's not meant for revenge against any of the issues presented or the characters involved. But I guess I need to take back saying this isn't about revenge, because it is about justice. And in some cases, justice and revenge go hand in hand. I am just trying to remove the hate from it, because hate usually fuels revenge. To get through this, you must love yourself. You need to be able to stand and look at yourself in the mirror, because without that, you won't make it. It's about my experience, what happened, and what I went through. It's meant for anyone in the same situation, looking for solutions they can relate to. Some will agree and say, "Spot on," and some will be far from what I am saying, but they can take bits and pieces to create their own solution and honestly, whatever works.

As much as I wish we could skirt around the subject, it's impossible. Healing is harsh, and it's something you cannot do without feeling pain and facing truths you never wanted to confront. It requires taking accountability after trauma and for the things you did to stay numb. This whole situation brought me to the peak of my alcoholism. I never realized I had a problem until the day I stepped into a room, four years after this situation, but that's a book for another time. My point here is not to blame my family for his actions, but for their own. You want so badly to point the finger and say everything is their fault, and how could they be such monsters? But although they might be, in their own ways, we can't forget those who carry trauma within themselves, which caused these reactions in the first place. You might not see it or realize that they are on the same trauma train as you because you just got on and didn't realize who else was on the ride but you will. And you will also be met with forgiveness for yourself and for them. Maybe that's too strong a word to use, because I haven't found forgiveness for everything yet, but more of an understanding, a viewpoint, that your healing has nothing to do with their healing.

Chapter two

I am Hispanic, and my family is from Mexico. I am American, and my parents are too, but the roots that run deep in this culture reflect struggles that so many of us face in all types of cultures, countries, and families. From what I have witnessed not just in my personal surroundings, but on the news and social media, it doesn't matter where you come from, what your background is, or what your religion is; these patterns come full circle, and we all share many similarities. Change is what we need. I can't speak about everyone's culture and religion, but I can speak about mine and my experiences.

I come from a mom and dad who had no business having children. Harsh? Not really. More people realizing this or seeking healing before continuous generational hurt is just raw and real. Not to mention, in my culture and family, the go-to saying is, "I'm your mother." It doesn't matter the mental illness, trauma, hurt, or abuse you're passing along if they are your mother. That's crazy talk! Anyone can have a kid. I could find a stranger on the street, have sex, and make a baby. It's wild that simply having a child seems to give some people permission to harm them. To not take care of them, or to have unrealistic expectations of them, like they were born into mistreatment, is emotionally and physically damaging, all to say, "I am your mother."

Being a parent is more than just creating a life. True parenting means love, protection, and healing yourself so you don't damage these innocent, precious kids. It's about making sure your partner is also well. Being a mother or father, a parent, is selfless if you do it the right way. It's about setting a good example. I am not saying "perfect," because we are human, but even as adults, we struggle to keep our emotions in check. Yet, in trying to look perfect for a photo or social media, we forget the little people who follow us as examples. They try to mirror our actions and emotions, which adults often fail at, especially those with unhealed trauma. Even healed adults have bad days and sometimes slip into negative habits instilled in them from childhood. Breaking deep-rooted patterns is an ongoing challenge.

I am concerned about the example we set when a partner does not actively participate as a parent or companion, yet we praise them as if they do. That was a problem in my experience, both in what I witnessed and what I eventually became guilty of myself. People have different reasons for this in each relationship, but I lived through it. As much as we may speak about disdain for someone or something, sometimes the negative influence we grew up with emerges within us. I am seeking solutions to ensure my children learn healthy models of love and partnership.

Before I had a partner, I realized that if I was going to do it alone or be mistreated, I still had a responsibility. My kids did nothing to deserve my bad decisions, yet the impact of my choices was imposed on them. I want to show my children that they must stand up for themselves, not let a man or woman belittle them, and choose the right partner or be alone. Both decisions, made wisely, come from self-love and are valid. I was not perfect. Before I got sober, I had a drinking problem. I was not a good friend, person, or mother. I was trying to drink away trauma, so I am not just a victim of my circumstances. But I realized I want my children to have better experiences than I did.

This realization took immense work, considering everything that happened to me as a child. My vow was that what happened to me would not happen to my children. They would never feel unloved or insecure. I often said about my mother, "I didn't think she ever wanted to be a mother, at least not to me." Sadly, after getting sober, I had amends to make to my son. His words were, "Mom, I know you love us and try so hard to take care of us and give us everything, but I didn't think you liked being a mom." His words killed my soul because I hadn't realized I was repeating the very patterns that hurt me.

Chapterthree

I think the manipulative part of all this is how loved my dad was and everything he did for his family, strangers, friends, colleagues, sisters, and mother, all vouching for him as if he were the best thing in the world. Even knowing, as adults, how wrong it was, I truly believe they did not realize how wrong it was. I think that, in the same way he treated me and my mother, he himself was gaslit, treated inappropriately, and raised by a mother who believed the bottle or a man was more important than her children. He was good at charming and loving you when needed, then turning around and hurting you physically and emotionally. That stems from the fact that they thought everything was normal and exactly how it should be. Yet they all had drinking problems from trying to numb things that, as a child, you do not really understand you are numbing. Taking it out on your own children is the entirety of this generational curse. It does not stop. You get bad habits instilled in you, trauma that was never yours, and you truly think it is normal.

I do understand that some evil stems from other evils, and then there are cases where someone is simply sick. There are great parents where it is a medical or chemical issue, but let us be real, that is so rare and far in between. I can say from my experience that this all comes from culture and generational abuse, that is it. The best explanation for his sisters and my aunts, most of them, not all, is this. When the news broke, they attacked me for doing the right thing, and to them it was wrong because all they ever knew was sweeping trauma and abuse under the rug. They mothered the same way they were taught. They reflected, as humans, in the best way they could. Do I believe they were evil? No. But it shows exactly what I believe, hurt people either hurt or heal.

It takes time, work, and therapy when you have been through something so deeply ingrained in your mind that you believe it is okay. As children, we trust the very people who are meant to love and protect us, and that is all we ever know. So how are we supposed to truly know that it is suffering, that it is damaging, and that it is wrong? It is abuse. It does not matter whether it is physical, sexual, or verbal, abuse is abuse. I believe my past was all I knew, so I did not realize how disgusting and wrong it was, not just for me, but for my brothers and my mother. The treatment was simply recycled, and for me, it was confusing on every level.

Now, as a parent and an adult, dealing with counseling, sobriety, and constant reminders is difficult. There are things I must witness within myself to see what happened and how to change it. Yelling uncontrollably at your child because they spilled something, getting angry because they cannot control a tantrum as a toddler when, as adults, we do not always control our own emotions, teaching a child that it is okay to yell at your spouse, to belittle, and that control is the only way to maintain control. These are mismatched emotions. This is not one sided, it applies to both genders and to humans in general. Letting your trauma affect your child and your relationships is the vicious generational cycle we keep repeating, and that is exactly why I am sharing my life events. It is not easy to release this type of information, but for so long I was damaged, afraid, and repeating the same generational trauma that I was terrified of and hurt by. I think the more people read about it and talk about it openly, the more it comes to light, and the more we, as wounded humans, can begin to heal instead of continuing to hurt from these experiences.

Chapter four

I remember as far back as when we lived in California. I was born and settled in Texas, but because of my dad's Marine history, which had so much to do with his ego and his excuses, we moved. Do not get me wrong, I am proud of the people who defend and care for our country and its people in the right way, but there is so much hidden behind that as well. People hide behind it, and he did in particular. I remember the days in California, living in a trailer park, and freedom was all I craved. If I could stay in the streets or at my best friend's house, I was fine. As a child, that should have been a red flag, doing everything possible not to be home, lying about my family and living situation, staying with people I barely knew, and it being considered acceptable by my family.

Like I said, as a mother, you realize so many things later that were never okay. The running, the hiding, parents allowing their child to stay with unknown people for days, even weeks. So many signs showed unfitness, but it is easy to look the other way. Thankfully, abuse never came from those friends' parents. I was lucky in that sense, and that is about it. People want to blame helicopter parents, but many of them are dealing with unhealed trauma that makes them fiercely protective at their core.

As a child, you do not know how wrong everything is, but instincts surface once you become a parent. Then you realize just how wrong it was, and you do everything to protect those babies. But what if you never have kids? What if you think nothing is wrong, or you feel it deep inside but cannot escape, and you do not talk about it because of the fear that was constantly forced on you? Can you imagine being with your partner for years, having a child with them, and never telling them your darkest moments? Never telling anyone, maybe only a few people who are no longer part of your life, or someone you trusted who told you to leave it alone or that it was not as bad as it seemed. Having the instinct to run and tell the law does not come naturally, and if it does, being so young and trying to make sense of something so unjust has a way of staying buried.

It is true insanity how real the effects of Stockholm syndrome, gaslighting, and grooming become in adulthood. My dad asked for kisses with tongue when I was a young child, all the time. My earliest memory of this was when we lived in California. Disgusting and wrong may be the first thing that crosses your mind now, but as a child, you are not processing it that way. What if you do tell someone, and they say, "Just do not say anything," or "He is drunk, stay out of his way"? Someone you trust and love. What if the very person doing it explains how special your bond is, how you are best friends, how your bond with them is stronger than with anyone else? Your sole provider and source of safety is telling you these things. As a child, probably around ten or eleven, and God knows what else happened before that, but this is all I remember, which therapists say is completely abnormal and likely tied to severe trauma blockage. How was I supposed to know it was not normal?

I had a neighbor, just a woman I met, and being a mom sounded so fun to her. She was young, probably between twenty and twenty five. Because she was nice, my parents let me have sleepovers with a stranger. She would tell them we were going to watch movies and eat snacks. She lived close enough that it was considered fine for me to cross wooden bridges to reach her mobile home. Can you understand that? As a parent, letting your child go to a grown person's home as if they know how to protect themselves or even understand right from wrong, especially when they are already experiencing abuse.

I remember staying at this woman's house. She did all the fun things, snacks and movies, but when it was time for bed, I was terrified. She would invite a boyfriend over, and I could hear them. I remember needing to use the bathroom, but I was too scared to ask. Instead, I laid on an air vent blowing heat to stay warm and dry. Moments like that make you realize how much your parents either did not want to be parents or did not realize how unsafe it was to put their child in that position, or that they believed the child would never say anything.

I understand it was the 1990s, but there was so much ignorance, and having children was treated as a requirement for success rather than truly living your own life and will. It is easy to call them monsters, but it is a vicious, disgusting cycle. All they were taught was success. Having children was how you became somebody or attached yourself to someone. In Mexican culture, you are nothing without family. When that mindset exists without healing or belief in therapy, abuse, physical or mental, that is where the recycled structure of pain and trauma comes from. You handle situations the way you were taught. This is my experience, not speaking for anyone else.

I saw my mother belittled. I saw my dad put his family before her. I saw him praised for mediocre care, praised as if he did his best. He worked hard, no doubt, that is all he ever knew how to do, and laziness does not tend to exist in this culture. Along with that, incest is normalized. Hiding a brother touching a daughter is swept away as if it is nothing. Dad, mom, grandpa, cousin, it all falls under the label of family, and family is protected. This culture does that. I am not saying all Hispanics do this, but this was my experience. After what happened and what was released on the news, many people came forward to me, and it appeared to be a pattern, this belief that family is everything and family must be protected, even from wrongdoing, the law, and evil.

That mindset is warped and creates a breeding ground for trauma to continue, to be passed down and unleashed onto the next generation of family members and children, continuing this deeply disturbed pattern.

Trying to remember every little thing is therapeutic. This all started as a journal while getting sober. Getting counseling has really helped me see that my passion and personality in seeking justice for everything I do or for the people I protect, stems from the desire and need to get justice for myself. Being left alone with an abusive dad who engaged in disturbing sexual behavior is trauma.

Wondering where my mother fits into all of this really hits deep. I remember when he would get drunk, and my mom was always trying to hide me. I wonder, why me? I have two brothers. What did she know that I didn't? It's so disturbing and hurtful to think about. She knew what kind of deranged person he was, but in the craziest way, it also brings up sympathy. I know some of you won't understand and want to scream, "Forget her and him!" Believe me, I'm working on feeling that way myself, but I also understand that in many of these situations and patterns, it stems from someone else.

I know my mother has been through some horrible things. No matter what she wanted or believed in as a child and growing up, she didn't have a say. Mom and dad knew everything, and everything she loved or wanted was considered wrong. That's a torment you will never understand unless you go through it. She had to be an adult for her siblings before she was an adult herself.

The resentment and anger you feel come from having to raise your own children while also raising someone else's. That will always disgust me. Your kids aren't here to help you raise something you created and chose to continue even without the means. What kind of child should have to do that? Yet, so many children go through it. The resentment is real. The hatred for having to endure that kind of life gets to you. I really think that's why my mom didn't care to have children or it became too much at one point because it was just work, from younger years to adulthood, to have that joy and love while being unselfish.

It's not for everyone, and it certainly shouldn't be forced. That's all she's ever known. As a kid, she didn't even make it to her first year of college, and she got pregnant. You might get mad at how selfish or "crazy" she seems, but can you blame someone whose life has been forced upon her? She didn't understand anything else or experience independence until her late 40s, and then she became codependent on her children. Thinking you are owed everything for being someone's mother because you gave birth to them ignores the fact that it takes the bare minimum to create a child. Anyone can do it; it's something most adults are capable of.

Having to go through that as a child, and then being thrust into the first man who comes into your life while your family pushes the idea of "be his wife and mother" as the only way to make something of yourself, is a very sad lie to live by. No dreams or ambitions are encouraged by your family, even if they see the dangers of this person, it's just how life continues. Your mother or father always siding with someone who hurts you, abuses you mentally or sometimes physically, is deemed acceptable because "he is the husband, the father of your children, he works."

When they took everything away to prevent you from being successful and independent, they also took away the mindset to love yourself or have confidence. This is why so many women are where they are today, it's continued generational trauma. The cycle of recycled actions in our culture shapes the lives we are expected to live. Thank God times are changing, but not enough. I still meet women today who excuse a man's abusive actions because he is their husband or the father of their child, because it's all they have ever known or been taught. The vicious cycle continues: the belittling, the insecurities, the struggle of finding yourself.

It's important to note that this is not one-sided. Men go through the same situations. They can be abused by their mothers. I use my own situation as an example, but this applies universally. A parent, man or woman, should not hurt, abuse, or make someone feel worthless and incapable of standing on their own. Being broken down is the exact hallmark of an abuser and narcissist. It's heartbreaking how deeply rooted hate for oneself can carry into the next generation.

The things my mother and father did to me are the same things that were done to them. My mother constantly felt she would never be good enough for her mother, yet she was at her beck and call. Her mother commanded, and she responded obediently, regardless of feeling belittled or inadequate, because that's all she was taught. The same happened with me. I was never skinny enough, I was always too fat, I could never be quiet enough, I fought too much, I wanted too much attention, everything was my fault. I would amount to nothing.

As a grown-up, in rare moments, my mother would say she was thankful I was nothing like her. Now, as an adult, despite the terrible things done to me by them, I am glad to have reached peace and realized it wasn't me. I was a child. Nothing is wrong with me; that's their problem. I am writing and sharing this because so many still wonder, "Why me? Why can't I be loved? What's wrong with me?" Sharing this may not fix everything, but it can spark the realization that change is needed, or that seeking help is important.

Chapter five

One of the significant moments that stuck with me and was constant in my home in California was my dad showing dominance and proving how "big and bad" of a man he was. I say that with quotes because, to me, a real man wouldn't put his hands on children or their spouse, or need to assert dominance by abusing or scaring those physically smaller than him.

My brother was just playing around and doing kid stuff in the living room. He ended up calling me a name, or a bad word, I don't even remember the word, but it was something like "idiot." I yelled, "Dad, my older brother called me an idiot!" He grabbed the VCR cable cords and started whipping him with them. My brother cried out loud, and it was horrifying. Then my mother took my brother to another room. My dad walked off and yelled at me, "Happy?" That's not what I meant at all. Honestly, as a kid, I didn't know what I wanted, but I knew it wasn't that.

My mom came out into the hall crying badly and yelled at me, "See what you did?" I felt so bad. I didn't realize then, because I was too young, how sad I was. I did feel like it was my fault, but it wasn't. What she meant was that this was her partner, her husband, doing this to her children. She should have left, but culture runs deep. In our upbringing, a man or husband especially a working one is untouchable. You are raised to believe that being a wife to a man is your everything, and in the Hispanic culture, that means following religion to honor the man. You are supposed to follow the Bible, but the man is allowed to sin, count his Hail Marys, and be as good as new. You let it go because he is still the husband, and you must obey.

I know it's sick, and anyone with a healthy, healed mindset would probably agree. But trauma and sickness run deep, so you can't always understand what someone is thinking. Sadly, some still agree with that stance, and I've seen it firsthand.

Being raised in the Hispanic culture as a Mexican, this is everything they believed in and continued. That doesn't mean every household was like this, or that it happens every time, but this is what happened in my life. It also happened before me, with my parents, their parents, cousins, family, friends, and everyone in our circle and surroundings as Hispanics. But it most definitely stopped with me.

When I was younger, he would hit me with objects or even his own hands, and he saw it as "discipline," which made it okay. At Anderson Elementary in San Jose, California, the nurse questioned my marks because they hurt. His go-to punishment was pinching my skin. I don't remember the exact reason I got them, but it was a red flag for the nurse, especially when I said my dad gave them to me for punishment. I guess breaking skin crosses that line because they called my mom and dad to ask questions. I got a lecture at home about how I could get taken away from them, and of course, being so young, they were everything to me as a child. I saw that as a bad thing and didn't mention it to the school again until later in this story, when I arrived in Texas and dealt with the nurse there.

With Mexicans, everyone is your Tía or Tío, which means aunt or uncle, and everyone is your cousin. I still truly believe you can build your own family because I had to deal with having none after all this. But you don't just trust someone because they are blood, Hispanic, or part of your culture when it comes to something so precious.

Before my dad came into money and his business, we lived in the trailer park in San Jose. My goodness, good old Magic Sands and I say that with complete sarcasm. The place held so many memories because I had too much freedom as a child, and it was such a fun place to explore. Of course, I got in trouble for not being where I said I was, climbing roofs, and being beyond adventurous. I was never afraid to try something new.

My dad liked to pull on my skirt or dress whenever I got caught doing something adventurous to "see if I actually had balls down there," as he so elegantly put it. He was rough about it, actually checking, and it was over anything even when I was outspoken because, according to him, only boys could love adventure, the outdoors, and speak up for themselves, right? There were times my mom would have to stop him, her sick expression showing how far overboard it had gone.

I remember so many neighbors from that place. We were gated all around but had a neighborhood inside. The pool and office with the community center were in the front, along with a gas station. To get in, you had to go through the Magic Sands sign entrance. That's where my parents met that older girl they let me stay with. The wooden bridge memory comes from crossing from street to street instead of going around; there were wooden bridges in the middle between houses.

One family we always had cookouts with was Hispanic as well. They lived around the block and had two daughters, one a year or maybe two older than me. She would always want to play house. She was the husband, and I was the wife. She would literally dry hump me and kiss me, acting like we were doing sexual things. I told my dad, and he just laughed, drunk, saying little girls are funny or maybe I took it wrong.

Now that I'm sharing this, I have no doubt in my mind that somehow she was being sexually abused. You don't just know stuff like that. I had to be a factor for her in some way, shape, or form. It didn't matter if it wasn't her parents, it could well have been exposure to her. When this happened, I was in third grade, eight or nine years old. What child would be doing or playing like that? Plain and simple, it wasn't playing. It was abuse. Her dad was creepy, he reminded me of an old-school vampire like Dracula and her mom, my goodness, I never witnessed a living figure in human form scream so suppressed.

The neighbor across the street from us was a lady who always left her kids with her older son. He was older than my brother. My brother was around twelve, so the older neighbor boy was thirteen or fourteen, a freshman in high school. The mom would leave all night, partying, dancing, drinking, maybe using drugs, and he literally took care of three other small kids. His brother had special needs, and then there was my age, plus two little sisters, one possibly four or younger, and a baby under two who always had to be carried.

We were all friends and hung out with the boys a lot, mainly the kid my age. The older kid had more responsibility and couldn't really hang out. I think he envied my brother because my brother lived like a normal kid, always on the street or having the next best game. When he was outside playing, he looked like a normal kid with no responsibility. I can't imagine how he felt with what he had to go through, but we didn't see behind closed doors, the hitting, the constant tearing down, and being told he was never good enough. Seeing it now as an adult, it is so sad. As kids, we are oblivious, and I thought it was cool he got to be an adult so young. Ironically, my parents would call the cops on her all the time when she was out all hours of the night.

The neighbors next door to them were two gay men. I never realized they were gay until we moved and I was showing pictures to friends. One friend said, "Oh, you have gay neighbors. My uncle has that same flag in his front yard." I was so surprised, but now I can see it in a stereotypical way. Both were very handsome, had the best yard and front porch, no kids, two cats, a beautiful, elegant home with nice material things, and were absolutely the most amazing, kind, fun people I ever met. I loved them dearly, and the memories of them always made me feel safe compared to what I had to experience with other neighbors and adults there.

On the other side of them was a mom with four kids. Facing them to the right was my best friend and her brother. She was younger than me by two years, but she was my best friend. We played all the time and had so many memories. Her trailer, however, no one was allowed in. It was absolutely disgusting, with trash piled in stacks so big that I called them "hills." One day, the police and social workers came and took her and her brother because of how unsanitary it was, and the way the mom constantly screamed at them raised red flags. Like I always say, we never know what is going on behind closed doors, but witnessing what we did outside was enough to bring fear for them. It broke my heart to hear her crying for her mom. It turned out the street got involved to have them removed, my parents included.

I now know the dangers of the environment she was in. It was absolutely disgusting, especially seeing it as an adult. My parents claimed she was irresponsible, and her husband allowed it as well.

One day, her mom came to my house and asked if they could take me to Six Flags because the little girl had a visitation with her foster parents. My parents said yes, of course. Looking back, I think they were trying to get rid of me. Unfortunately for them, I am a survivor, lol. I kid, but honestly, I was put in situations I shouldn't have been in. I remember being scared in their car, but thankfully, it was a good trip. I cried hugging her goodbye after a long day. I was very lucky they were so kind to me and took me. But what kind of parents, after all they witnessed and said, would let their under-ten-year-old child go with them?

I don't know the exact age because our neighbors rotated. The gay couple moved to a house, so someone else took over their trailer: a weird lady with a very young son I ended up watching a lot, I'll get into that later. The girls' parents moved as well, and then the "bad mom with four kids" moved too. She probably got sick of having the cops called on her because she would rather party than be a mom.

But before she moved, something huge happened. Her son had me alone in the house while she was gone. He was not supposed to have anyone over, but he snuck me into the back to show me something. He took me to his mom's room and started showing porn on the TV, soft porn that came in and out on the cable, probably a channel he didn't have, but sometimes it would pop up. He said it was what he and I were supposed to be doing. He literally grabbed my shorts and tried to take them off. He put his hand under my shirt and kissed all over my face. I yelled stop and he started crying and begged me, "Please, we have to do this…"

Chapter six

I remember getting mad, yelling no again, and pushing him. I ran the hell out of there. I don't know why I didn't tell anyone maybe because I felt so bad for him. I had seen his mom abuse him, hit him, yell at him, and treat him like absolute trash, and she even allowed her boyfriends to mistreat him. That lady was an absolutely sick excuse of a parent. I knew that much even as young as I was.

I had told my dad things before, and he always made my mom seem like the enemy. I see now that it was a tactic of his, part of the grooming in my upbringing. But my mom never tried to intervene. She never questioned or asked where I was for so damn long. And even if I did explain or answer, it was so easy for her to just say okay and move on with her life. As a mother, I couldn't imagine not being there for my kids, protecting them, and making sure they were safe in every aspect.

She treated me differently from my brothers, like a house divided. I had my dad, and my brothers had my mom. My older brother received most of the abuse from my dad, so my mother protected him. I really can't tell you what happened with my little brother. Like I said, I almost only remember me and my older brother, living in California, and maybe it was because my little brother was too small, but all the situations I remember always involved just me and my older brother.

Back to that horrible lady, my mom. I remember all the times my parents mentioned that she lived off welfare and kept having kids so the government would take care of her. I didn't understand what they meant at the time, but I do now.

The older boy who did that to me ended up in a fistfight with my brother. I don't know what it was over, but they fought a lot. I know my brother was genuinely aggressive and mean to that boy, and given what I know he's been through now, God only knows what the hell was happening back then.

Before they moved, the boy's mom lost her 12-year-old babysitter and housekeeper. He was in high school as a freshman, got kicked out, and was arrested by the police for making a hit list of people he wanted to kill at his school. Someone found it. He went to Santa Teresa High School, but the sad thing is that looking back, getting out from under that POS "mom" was probably the help he needed. Being taken away from her was likely the best thing that could have happened to him. But with how long ago it was, and the way mental illness and abuse were handled back then, I'm sure they didn't take any of that into consideration. They just saw him as the villain who needed to be put away.

I remember my dad joking that he bet my older brother was top three on that hit list, along with his best friend, because they were always mean to him. Now, after therapy, counseling, and sobriety, I can't say it enough: a lot of trauma isn't evil, it's just known, taught, and recycled. But we get to a point where we either do better than the trauma that hurt us, or worse, and sometimes there's a time when you're actively choosing to stay evil.

After everything I've been through, I still love hard and see the good in people. I've had some mishaps, but I see the good in so many people who have been through trauma as well. I see it in my older brother, the love and kindness he shows and the way he tries so hard to be part of something.

My younger brother doesn't understand what he's been through and probably never will. My mother does a good job of playing the victim and feeding my brothers very different versions of each other. I don't know what it does for her, or maybe it doesn't expose the manipulation she's done within all of us, but it doesn't matter. My point is that my little brother lived a very different life than us. Honestly, I think witnessing things he couldn't understand as a child put him in the spotlight to be the golden child: never get in trouble, make good grades, obey mom and dad at all costs.

Not to mention my older brother and I were stupidly aggressive, with misplaced anger in every way. We took it out on each other. My older brother often attacked my little brother, and even if I defended him, he always showed submission to our older brother. Not me, I would still fight my hardest and continue to start conflicts with him, especially over my little brother. That experience, however, helped me never be afraid to stand my ground in the future. It was both a good and bad thing for me.

Because my little brother saw what we went through, he thought we were just bad kids constantly being punished. To him, the way to avoid what we went through was to be a good kid. I don't blame him for not understanding, given what he was fed and experienced. He is amazing and accomplished. He's smart and educated, but ignorant and oblivious to the abuse, trauma, and enabling my parents perpetuated.

I, on the other hand, witnessed the abuse firsthand. There are people out there who will say my little brother was the best person to walk the planet, that's what narcissists do. There are always two visions: one for the show and one behind closed doors. Nothing my older brother and I went through, he experienced. What my mom feeds him, he can't comprehend, because he wasn't exposed to as much as we were. My older brother is just trash to him, and he can't understand him. Myself included, I am always considered a liar, nothing, and my mom has to help me even when I've been the only one helping her for years. My little brother doesn't understand why my mom "deals" with us.

The beauty of getting help and staying sober is that I have nothing to prove to my "family." It's not my little brother's fault, or other family members who get fed the nonsense. She does nothing to help my older brother out of his trauma, so he will never understand she's the cause. Even with court, jail, and my dad trying to run him over, he wants to be loved by his father. It means so much to him because he has never dealt with the reality that his abuser was his dad, and my mom not protecting or helping him in a healthy way makes her just as much his abuser.

When you are abused that badly, you are stuck in the same trauma you experienced. My big brother still sees me as the same lying 12-year-old who always got him in trouble, no matter what I have done, sobriety, career, or even what I have done for him. He has been enabled, and in his head, it's earned or deserved. It will always be forgiven because it's "mom" and "dad," without realizing they caused all the pain. Delusion and abuse run deep when you're too scared of change.

Like most abuse victims, and if you've never been through it, you just don't understand it. This is the exact concept. People abused by a mom, dad, step-parent, uncle, cousin, family friend, or anyone in the family, no matter what the abuse, molestation, rape, or otherwise, act hysterical, sad, and emotionally destroyed when the abuser passes, as if nothing ever happened. Especially when the abuse was groomed at a young age, loyalty runs sickly strong. God knows why. To a normal person, it can make you sick, but trying to understand it means trying to explain why these people acted the way they did.

It's such an emotional and mental rollercoaster. It's so wrong, and I couldn't understand it. Now that I am better, sober, and working to understand what happened to me mentally, while also accepting the physical part, I can share it. It helps me understand it's ingrained in us, but it still feels wrong. That's why you feel so messed up, you feel it's wrong, yet you're doing it or having sympathy for that abuser.

The most messed-up part is that I would have cried too if my dad died before he was arrested or even right after. But when he got his sentence, I was happy. I was surrounded by such amazing support, it felt good and none of it was blood family. It was friends turned family. My actual blood family, especially on his side, made sure I felt bad about telling the truth, posting threats on social media. I even had to write the DA asking what I could do because it was public with threats against my kids, the very people and supposed family exposed to the same sick abuse.

When I saw my mother break down over him and his sentence, and she didn't even make court appearances, it almost felt wrong. I still had sympathy and wondered if I had made a mistake, even with all the work, evidence, and confidence it took to get there. That's the messed-up cycle of trauma and mental abuse, it can make you feel crazy and wrong for doing the right thing.

At the time, I wasn't sober, and I "healed" the pain with alcohol. After defending a child and winning in court, never having healed from my past, it was one of the darkest times of my drinking, with three babies to care for and my past and present colliding with this national news crime.

Chapter seven

Getting back to the Magic Sands crew. I know you're thinking what the hell was happening to that place, and I would say it was a trailer park thing, but as life continues, you start to understand that's not the only reason for it, or at all. Honestly, I met some of the best people in that trailer park. My next door neighbor to our right was around 70, and her husband was probably in his 80s. He passed away while we lived there, and I went to the funeral, and she stayed our neighbor and ended up either in a home or with family, but she sold her trailer a year before we left, I think, or around that time. She was amazing, beautiful, so sweet, everything a Hallmark next door grandmother could be. White hair, white little old lady. She always let us over. She introduced me to Judge Judy and Jerry Springer, some good stuff back then. It had to be the 98/99 era, maybe even the 2000s. We moved from California to Texas in the middle of my 6th grade year. One of the crazier neighbors and memories, which I wouldn't say was horrible like the others, but a big family moved into the very corner space. I won't mention names or major descriptions of certain things. I could care less about my own truths out, but I will allow others to reveal themselves or give those Facebook detectives a run for their money. Lol, back to it. We always loved the corner lot because you could play right next door to the opening there, and my parents called that family the hillbillies. The lady that took over the gay couple's home had a little boy. My mom would let me stay there all the time. I'd watch over him and play games all the time. He was so sweet and precious and always wanted to play with toys. He had to be about four. A couple weeks, maybe months into it, he changed a lot. He started always closing his eyes. He kept wanting to "kiss," like be a lot more loving in the touchable sense, always hugging. I could myself tell something was off, even as a child. One play date, he was pulling out his penis, just out of his pants. That's the only time I felt off, and I went home and told my mom. I'm sure now, as a parent of a little boy, that wouldn't seem so crazy. It's a boy. They love to be naked. But for me as a kid, and with all the other stuff, and he's never done it, it made me feel really uncomfortable, and he changed. He really did in personality. Right before that happened, maybe a couple days prior to the changes, the corner neighbors my parents referred to as "hillbilly" and the lady with the son got into it in the middle of the street. Like head to head, the girl that lived in the corner home, her, her parents, and the lady screaming at each other, saying things like "your daughter is sick," "I'm calling the cops," back and forth yelling. But I don't remember the cops actually showing up, but my parents made us go inside, and we had no idea what was happening. They might have, but I didn't. But now, adding up to the boy's behavior and actions, it made sense what she ended up telling my mom. The boy had to be 4 or 5. My mother went over to talk to the lady and explain how I felt and what was happening, which wasn't like my mom to ever come to my defense. My dad always acted like the hero when it fit his agenda, but while she was talking to the boy's mom, I was on the side stairs listening, and I heard the lady said the little girl touched her son. She caught her touching him, sucking on his private areas, and that the little girl was only 10, and basically everything she did to her son, and none of them were to be anywhere near the little boy, and warning my mother not to let me or my brothers play with that girl. That's the last I remember of them or the family and hanging out so much with anyone from that place. I was going into 6th grade, more friends, more sleepovers. I practically lived at my best friend's house from the 5th grade, like always there, and it was normal to be away from my family at a constant, or I was always at my cousin's house, which was normal compared to my parents' home.

My parents, being how they were, I had too much freedom, or things I would tell them, it was like I said nothing at all, or maybe they thought I was lying or wanted to pretend I was. Why face the stuff you're dealing with? Also, with all this and what I do remember, I'm sure there's so much more dark, sick shit, but I remember in spots. I also talked to a therapist that said my spotty memory is just not normal, that I don't remember my little brother from California, and I can't remember a lot of things from that whole stage. But what I do, the names and people are so vivid I could recall street names and locations and see it perfectly. I remember one of my dad's best friends, and he was known as my Tio. I don't remember much of him or his name, but I do remember him having a teenage son, and he always wanted to kiss me or love on me. They never had a problem leaving us alone for a long time. I remember one time we were playing doctor, and my dad walked in. I was thankful. It was so uncomfortable. It was him and his older brother, and they were touching on me and checking me like a play doctor. I was thankful he was going to get mad, and he didn't. He just said it was time to go home. He had been watching the fight and drinking, and he asked me what I was playing, and I said doctor, and he was so calm about it. I felt like I did something wrong, but he never acted like it. It was just like the time with the girl that humped me. I really wonder what was going on. My dad would always have people over for the game, and he had friends over that were Mexican and only spoke Spanish. They lived in the trailer park too, but much farther away, the farthest side. Well, one time, one took me on his bike and told me my dad said it was okay. I remember waiting in his room, and he changed in front of me like nothing. I felt so off and wrong, and the last thing I remember is flashes like a camera and his jeans and belt buckle, and then coming home. He drove me back, and my dad just acted so normal, waiting on the porch, but scolded me for not telling him before I left. I was under 12! Weird shit like that happened constantly. Sometimes I couldn't tell if it was real or a dream. I went through my dad's computer once, and under his folder, Juanito, under it was porn, but weird cartoon porn, and it always looked like grown men with a little girl, but in anime. So because it was a cartoon, child porn was okay? I didn't realize it till later and talking with someone about my entire history after court and being sober, but it's things like that made me realize I was abused. My older brother now shows signs he was, and that family would hide anything from anyone, and that's my memories of California. A therapist also told me, from what I shared, they could put my face into a child porn database if I ever wanted to check facial recognition and see if I'm a part of that, and I refused! I am still scared now to do something like that. With everything I know, I don't doubt it's a possibility with all this shit, and there's so much more I could say, but those are the main points and situations I was put in at such a young age and what's coming to light now, what is wrong and how this culture and family will keep anything from anyone as long as you're the husband and man and providing for the family.

Chapter eight

My parents and family labeled me a liar, and I was one, because my first instinct was to hide or avoid being hit, since that was what punishment meant. I followed their lead, believing it was always better to lie about being better than to actually achieve it, yet they would have no idea where I picked up these bad habits. I believe that as a child, you learn from your parents, partnerships, and habits, good or bad, and most of your characteristics come from home. There is a small percentage of children who are naturally "bad" from the start, like one in a million, but don't feed me that nonsense, kids pick up behavior at home from their parents. Yes, there is curiosity, learning curves, and figuring things out on your own, but your child primarily learns from you and what you and your partner model in your home if you have a full family. Single parents, you are the example. Parents together, children are watching how you treat each other, how you divide responsibilities, and how you handle things together and separately. I will stand by that until the day I die. From my experience and that of my siblings, it is what I stand on, and it is why breaking generational curses is so significant, because that is what they are and all we know. It is very difficult to break them, especially after having children of your own.

I am strong because of them, and I improved because of them. I hated how much I hated myself for what was done to me and for how I repeated the same harmful patterns that were inflicted on me. Emotional abuse is real, and you often do it without realizing it, having been on the receiving end for so long. You can hate something your parents did to you and still catch yourself doing it unintentionally. One of the hardest truths I had to accept, and apologize to my children for, involved verbal abuse. It was always so extreme. Being Hispanic, Mexican, screaming was the default, belittling in every way, and yelling as if you had committed the worst mistake of your life, even for simple accidents. This warped your perception of yourself as an adult.

We were always fearful of getting in trouble, even for accidents. My brother would beg if I said I was going to tell on him, which is natural for a child, but the punishments were always severe. My older brother received the worst of it. I can't recall much about my little brother's role in our life or home in California. I have a small memory of him cutting all my Barbies' hair, but he didn't get punished the same way. Occasionally he might have been disciplined, but if so, it was always blamed on me and my older brother. Once, my mom punished him because my older brother and I refused to admit to something that had broken. She sent us all to our rooms, except my little brother went to our parents' room. He took the punishment quietly while my older brother and I hollered, doing everything loud children do. Little brother fell asleep crying. My mother said she couldn't believe we allowed him to take the punishment, but as kids, we didn't care and were trying to save our own skin from unjust punishment. These are two vivid memories that show how he was treated differently. A sibling can live a very different experience in the same abusive home.

I remember my cousins the most. Escaping to their homes always felt better than my own. I got my period in the fifth grade, and I was terrified. My mom always said it was disgusting and that I should be ashamed. She also constantly claimed I was too sexual for my age, as if getting my period meant I was boy-crazy. I now understand that this shame stemmed from the traumatic experiences I endured. When I tried to tell her, she was mortified. She said I was too young, and that only sexual girls got their periods. I had no understanding or balance because of my upbringing and abuse. I ended up telling her I was just kidding and didn't have it because I was too young. I didn't know how to manage it properly and would use socks as makeshift pads, inspired by a show I had seen where a girl did the same. People would call that disgusting, and that was my life. I felt deep shame for something natural and hid it. It wasn't until we moved to Texas that I got proper pads and tampons, learning from friends. I cried so hard the first time and never spoke to my mother about it again. Now, as a mother, I cannot imagine shaming my daughters for something natural.

She always shamed me for shaving as well. When I tried to do it myself, I nicked myself and bled in the shower. She came in and acted as if I was committing a mortal mistake. Her explanation made me feel I was going to die over something minor. She was not reassuring but controlling, likely because my father, in his own sick way, favored me. Somehow she blamed me or accused me of stealing his attention. This is how corrupt and generational these dynamics can be. As a woman in the Hispanic culture, you are taught to serve and obey your father, brothers, and any male figure in your home. They are treated as leaders and the law. My personality and spirit could never conform to that, and that is why I was punished and considered the "bad" child. I was loud, sexual, disobedient, and "wrong."

I only started shaving on my own because all the girls in my class wore dresses, and they made fun of my hairy legs. I told my mom, and she became angry. She insisted I was too young for personal hygiene. Now, I am very intentional with my daughters about explaining personal hygiene, how natural it is, and why anyone who shames that is wrong. Teaching a child to care for themselves is basic and essential.

I could not go to my mother about anything. She never had the sex talk with me. My father did, but it was the most ignorant explanation imaginable. He sat me down in the kitchen in California, demonstrated with his hands how a penis goes into a vagina, and then laid out a glass of milk, saying that's how much sperm goes in and it stays for two weeks, and you will get pregnant. He reminded me of the idiotic coach in the movie Mean Girls, who implies, "You have sex, you will die." I took that "educational" talk with a grain of salt. That was how things were handled in the house.

Even punishments, he would take me to the other room, make me remove my shorts and underwear, and then pretend to spank me. He would bend me over and say, "I'm not really going to spank you, but don't tell your mom," as if he were the hero, the good guy, because I didn't get spanked. But what he got to look at and make me do was wrong. I know that now, but at the time, I really thought, wow, what a great dad, not spanking me when I'm in trouble. In other cases, it was the "give me a kiss with tongue if you really love me." I had no idea how sick and wrong it was. I was a child. I didn't know any better or what was happening. It makes me so sad to realize how badly I was taken advantage of, in the same house with the same woman who left me alone constantly with him. Maybe she didn't know, just maybe, but when he did get mad, he would use the belt on us, his hands, or objects, no problem.

I think, in my culture, they believe you are allowed to treat your child however you see fit. I do understand disciplining a child, but what I don't understand is this: you wouldn't hit your boss. You wouldn't hit your significant other or you're not supposed to, as an adult. You can't physically discipline your friends, either. But we are allowed to do these things to children and still expect them to become normal, functional adults in society. That's ridiculous. The emotions we experience as children shape who we become as adults.

My mom just couldn't understand why I always got in fights. I was just a bad, angry kid that seemed to steam up out of nowhere. I was born into disappointment, and nothing or no one around me, including the people raising me, contributed to helping that. LOL, that's sarcasm. I know you sometimes catch on to sarcasm through a book.

Chapter nine

My dad, and everything he was taught, came from an abuser as well. It usually does, which is why understanding everything is so important. That's why I say over and over: you are what you are taught at a young age. If it's all you've ever known, how do you even understand what's wrong? And all these parents in denial, wanting to just blame the kids those "parents," to me, are dealing with their own sick problems. But the ones who can get help and heal, that's who this is reaching out to. Those who want to change generational trauma and not continue it because of their own misery, those are the people this is for. Maybe it even flips your mind to understand how it keeps going if we allow it. But there was a time I wanted something different and let my shame, drinking, or other things take over, so I understand, it's not easy.

My dad's mom was abusive. He admitted in court that he had been sexually abused as well, which he said led to his gay tendencies. To me, his defense is disgusting. I think he claimed that being gay made him do those things, which is just a reflection of his Catholic and Mexican cultural mindset of blaming everything but himself, blaming sin or shame rather than his own choices. The culture is stuck in the past, and the Bible says it's a sin. I have such a problem with that because I love God. My faith is number one, and it helped me get here. But I don't believe the way people interpret scripture. I believe the Bible teaches kindness, selflessness, and other good characteristics.

I believe if you treat any human being with kindness, and they respond in kind, you mind your own business, and it will show you how amazing life can be, instead of getting caught up in the misery of judging others. The Bible says, "Let those who have never sinned cast the first stone," one of my favorites. Just because you sin differently doesn't give you the right to judge someone's lifestyle. There are certain things I have opinions about, but I am speaking here about good humans being treated badly when there is no right to judge them, or using religion as an excuse to avoid accountability for crimes.

I think Jesus showed growth, love, and kindness, washing the feet of sinners and welcoming them regardless of their past or current sins. That's showing that God is light. That's why I love my faith: because I know that, through addiction, alcoholism, and true healing, I can become a better person despite my past and what I was doing to myself and others. I can redeem myself by following the example Jesus set.

Following the Old Testament rules, where people threw rocks and judged others, I'm not on board with that. Obeying your husband and all his sins because you're married especially in this day and age, when people get married with barely any time to know each other, while battling codependency and lacking boundaries, is not acceptable. If he is mentally or physically abusive and has never healed, you cannot prioritize his authority over your children or your own safety. Selling a 14-year-old into marriage for farm animals, again, not on board. I'm going far back, but I try to focus on change and not judging past mistakes.

I strive to be like Jesus, leading people to know Him through love, not judgment, and by showing kindness. That's how I live. I don't judge anyone for how they live, their religion, their life, or whom they love. If someone is good to me, that's what matters.

The problem I saw with my dad and many others in my family was how they were raised. I could have easily been the same. He believed he could do no wrong. Instead of being like Jesus, people tend to think they are Jesus, with the right to judge and belittle others, often without realizing it. That is why people can hate organized religion. I saw my parents sit in church every Sunday while still living through what I endured. I don't know how I still came to love my faith so deeply, but I am thankful for it because when that was all I had, it truly helped me survive and strive to do better.

Regarding my dad blaming his abuse on being gay, being gay does not mean someone will molest a child. Anyone with sick tendencies could commit abuse, regardless of sexual orientation, religion, or culture. That is an individual problem, a moral and legal failure. His actions prove he was sick, not because he liked men, but because of his constant need to hurt and abuse.

He made my mother do so many sick things, revealing them to me later, thinking we were best friends. Mentally, she was conditioned to obey. Being around a narcissist long enough, you eventually turn into one yourself. You either continue the cycle of hurt or ensure that you and those around you never go through it again. Surviving doesn't always mean living. Surviving takes strength. It also means surviving the mental chaos of what you naturally learned or were conditioned to do.

My mother used to be the victim, then turned it into her advantage to get her way. She allowed evil to continue because of what she was taught. She is always in church, always quoting the Bible, but she doesn't see past her own judgment. She may defend a child molester because she never experienced protection from her parents or a man. She grew up a survivor, but hurt people hurt or heal. There's no in-between. It's instinctual to hurt others like we were hurt, or to heal and do right for ourselves and others.

When I say she had no fighting chance, I mean in terms of personality. Everyone is built differently. To believe you must stand by someone committing heinous crimes simply because they are your husband takes a toll. Repetitive mental abuse, combined with lifelong conditioning from family, is itself a form of abuse. Her mother told her to stand by a child abuser. One of her sisters even called me and said, "You know if this was your kid's dad, you'd stand by his side." Negative, gross girl. I left him for less. He may not have seemed monstrous in every detail, but all of it circulates back to trauma for all of us.

I think my mom may have wanted to leave him for herself but couldn't disappoint her family. Doing the right thing takes everything you have. Even if it's the right choice, you have no idea about the turmoil involved. I experienced the same. Doing the right thing comes with shame, shame from following what you were taught with "family," or shame for doing right. Nothing is sadder than feeling shame for doing right, but that's normal, right? Family before the law, before abuse. Some people likely just felt shame saying that alone.

Chapter ten

In all of this, you might want to hate my mother. God knows, I thought I did for so long. I am still hurt and angry, there's no doubt about that, but the peace I have knowing she has no hold on me anymore outweighs any other feeling toward her. This very hatred, however, is what keeps people from moving forward. It allows something so broken to consume us, turning us into the very characters we claim to hate. When I speak about change, that means accepting that these very humans we cannot understand, and "hate," are experiencing nothing but the same cycles.

It reached a point where someone who hurt me so much, the person I "hated", was mirrored in my own life when my child told me he knew I took care of him, but he didn't think I was happy to be a mom. That is where the hurt gets real and messy because I love being a mother, yet that was the very same thing I felt about my own mom.

My mother, from a young age, was convinced her only role in life was to be a wife, to answer to a man who, because he worked a basic job and provided basic necessities, which we could have provided for ourselves, was seen as her savior. That is what this culture does. Being a Mexican woman, that is exactly what I experienced, as did my mother and her mother. The idea that his sins can be forgiven simply because he is the man, the head of the household, was passed down. In the same way her mother did not protect her, this mistreatment of women in Hispanic culture becomes a cycle of generational trauma.

The number of times I witnessed my mother being humiliated, shamed, and belittled is staggering. I truly cannot believe I am here today, standing my ground and achieving what I have. That is the purpose of me sharing these grim truths: to break my generational curse, family trauma, and abuse, and to help anyone who can take pieces of this to prevent themselves from going through the same experiences.

This underscores the seriousness of having children with the wrong partners and exposing them to toxic dynamics, while believing "two parents are better than one." From my personal experience, such thoughts are a toxic mindset. Children witnessing the mistreatment of another human being, stemming from unresolved trauma of one or both parents, are inevitably affected. Even with how far I have come, you cannot understand the sadness, the unhealthy coping mechanisms, the heartbreak, and the neglect of my body, mind, and character, including the abuse of alcohol and substances to numb the pain.

The vicious cycle continues when a parent does not protect their child and follows the societal notion that "two parents are better than one," perpetuating generational mistakes. Children witnessing mistreatment and unresolved trauma from a parent onto another parent are set up for failure. They learn to emulate the very behaviors that hurt them, developing insecurity, disrespect, and patterns of harmful behavior. Once again, it all ties back to upbringing, culture, religion, and the many things imposed on us from a young age.

I am not trying to lecture or parent adults. I am speaking only to protect children, including my own, because I am still managing the fallout in my kids' lives and addressing character traits they picked up from me while I healed. I am speaking about what I witnessed, and despite it all, I do believe in healthy families and love.

I recognize that this book is not for everyone. Some people never need to break a generational curse. They inherit culture and heritage that celebrates beauty, goodness, and love, and they recycle that positive experience for their children. That is a truly beautiful way of life. Unfortunately, I grew up surviving, not thriving in love, so my perspective is more protective and aggressive than nurturing. I am learning to change that by spending time with my children and their father. However, he has his own trauma. Together, we had little chance to love ourselves or each other because all we knew was trauma, abuse, and addiction.

The idea of saving someone when you cannot save yourself is poetic but unrealistic. You cannot truly love another if you do not love yourself. Stories and romance movies often celebrate this myth of salvation through love, but the reality is, healing must come first. His father repeatedly chose relationships over his children, prioritizing partners over his own children. His mother, often on and off drugs, chose addiction over her son for most of his life. That alone, combined with all the trauma that followed, informs much of this book.

Hurt people either hurt or heal. If you repeat the patterns of your parents without healing, it does not make you evil, it makes you unhealed and stuck in pain. Therapy taught me that many people from abusive or traumatic backgrounds repeat patterns unconsciously. His father, however, did try to show a different model as a grandfather. Grandparents sometimes attempt to atone or grow, and I allow him a lighter responsibility with my children because I love having that. Like many unhealed people, he does not believe in therapy, and his partner does not either. Without healing yourself, you continue to repeat cycles of pain. That is why I intervene for my children. I will do anything to protect them from the same harm we endured, regardless of words or enablers, because actions speak louder than words.

Chapter eleven

Texas. We left California when I was 12. I was born in Texas and lived there for a while before traveling because my dad was a Marine. We stayed in California for years, and then my parents decided to move back to Texas. We left in the middle of my sixth-grade year, around the age of 12. I was miserable. I had so many friends, whom I loved dearly, likely more than most 12-year-olds, because I often used them as an escape. I stayed with them for long periods, probably for reasons I have already described. My parents seemed unconcerned about their young child spending so much time away from home, not even with family.

We drove from California to Texas once our trailer sold, and they found a house in Texas. They did not tell us until the week of the move. My parents rented a U-Haul, with my dad driving it and my mom driving the minivan. We stopped at hotels along the way. The U-Haul could fit only one passenger, so I sometimes drove with my dad. As always, he made things uncomfortable by bringing up inappropriate topics, which I did not recognize as wrong at the time.

Any normal, well-raised person should be disturbed and scared by experiences like this. Being touched or kissed by an adult or family member inappropriately, being told to kiss longer or with tongue, is disgusting. I did not know better. I thought my dad was my best friend in the world, and he made sure it seemed that way. Even looking back, I wish as a child, and now as a parent, that I had understood the wrongness of it.

He would even grab one of my little cousins by the face to kiss her directly, mouth to mouth, while she cried and screamed. He was drunk and taunted her on the stairs, insisting that she, as his niece, had to show him affection. His sister, her mother, would laugh and find it appropriate. These are the things you witness as a child and are told to ignore. Even with a cousin screaming in fear, it was deemed "okay" because he was drunk. In a Mexican family, being drunk often acts as a free pass, a literal get-out-of-jail card.

I can't explain it, but I didn't realize until he was arrested and I began counseling that he had always been grooming me. He would always tell me that we had private conversations and secrets because we shared a bond. He made it seem like my mom didn't care about me the way he did, and he used my fears against me, whether or not they were true. With everything that's happened, I can't even say for certain that they weren't. He would act as if I were his favorite child, so special and his only girl, while simultaneously belittling me and my personality. He said my brothers were mean to me because of the special love he showed me, and they were jealous.

One time, while driving somewhere, we were talking about my friend and her mom. My dad had met her mom in college, and we often went over to their house. He mentioned that he was going to miss them, and I said I would too, that the daughter was so much fun and it was always a blast. Then he told me that, because I was his best friend and he trusted me so much, he wanted me to know that he was having sex with her mom. He said he had to tell me because he couldn't tell anyone else, and I somehow understood him. He claimed my mom never gave him enough sex and didn't do her job as a wife. He told me that if I ever got married, I needed to understand the importance of pleasing my husband sexually, and that it was a woman's most important job, along with cleaning and raising the children. He said that when someone isn't getting what they need, it would make a man stray out of desperation, because his wife wasn't doing her job. He portrayed her as the villain to justify his actions.

What's shocking is that I usually sided with my dad or believed what he told me. Later in my own relationships, I realized I had internalized putting a man's needs before my own, though that eventually changed. At the time, I just cried uncontrollably. I felt so bad for my mother, seeing all she had done to care for us, even with her flawed sense of parenting. I just cried and said, "You cheated on my mom. You had an affair!"

Chapter twelve

I couldn't stop crying. He said he was sorry, that he told me because he felt I needed to know for my own sake and because he considered me his best friend. He explained that he had been with her everywhere, even when I was at playdates with my friend. He was a hypocritical excuse for a man. He claimed it was important to be a wife and obey your husband, yet cheating was somehow acceptable if it suited his desires. Only the man had validation; a woman doing the same thing was labeled a slut, a betrayer, or worse.

At the time, I didn't know what a narcissist or abuser was. I was 12, maybe 13, a child. As much as I want to kick myself now, everyone always says, "You were a kid. It was your father. How could you have known?" That's the shame you carry even to this day. Writing this book has been draining. It started as therapeutic, and as I pieced everything together, I realized how much shame is attached to doing the right thing when you were raised to hide the truth and pretend it wasn't happening.

Even after the arrest, I would question myself. Years later, through trauma and counseling, I realized it shouldn't have been a surprise. I had assumed it was "me," and that our bond was real. Only through counseling and writing this book, redoing it sober, did I truly understand. Previously, my journal was simply a place for anger, truth, and release. The national news and headlines wanted only the gruesome details. Thankfully, falling in love with my children gave me the strength to fight for any child, even myself, the child who was never protected or defended. I vowed never to repeat that cycle. My children are the reason I could love myself and stand up for others facing the same demons and cultural corruption I did. When this story hit the news, the outpouring of messages I received made me realize how many people are told to sweep abuse under the rug: "It's family. No one will believe you. Don't forget they take care of everything." No one considers the toll on the child. That cycle continues, and we keep reliving it.

Chapterthirteen

By middle school, I didn't care about myself or my body, and I thought giving myself to people sexually was how you gave love. I sought attention from older men and even flirted with teachers; some flirted back. I was labeled "a ho" for the way I sought attention, even though I didn't have sex with these boys. Rumors made me seem like the worst, as if I were sexually active in school bathrooms while still a virgin. I didn't care about clearing up the rumors because I didn't care about myself enough to care what anyone else thought.

The girls who spread rumors hated me because I reflected the pain I carried, and my actions were misinterpreted. I had no boundaries not because I didn't want them, but because I didn't know what they were. Girls hated me because their boyfriends sought my attention, and I gave it, thinking it would make me accepted or popular. I wouldn't tell their girlfriends; I would protect their secrets. That was the loyalty I had been sickly taught.

After all the counseling and healing, I now embrace being a "girls' girl," because women never protected me or saw me as worthy. Now, as a human being, I stand for love, respect, and advocating for those who deserve better. My extroverted nature allows me to connect, but I also learned that others' actions often reflect their own issues, not mine. Narcissists, however, exploit opportunities to manipulate, which is why standing up for oneself and others especially children is vital.

My father always pinned me against my mother, blaming her for everything. She could never be pleased; she was always criticized, and everything became my fault. Ironically, he often called her a narcissist, when his own actions clearly shaped her reactions. Anyone can misuse that label, but actions speak louder than words. Observing what someone does reveals the truth, ACTIONS SPEAK LOUDER THAN WORDS.

She got bitter, and I know it was because of him, but at what point do you get sick of what he is doing and protect your kids? I will never understand that. Like my son says, "we just are not built that way," and thank all the stars for that. She would say she got lucky with my brothers, but not with me. She even told me she only wanted boys, and I felt that to be true the entire time. I "joked" to everyone that my dad had an affair and I was the product of that, and that my real mom was gone, and that is why my "mom," or stepmom, hated me and treated me differently, and sadly no one ever thought I was lying.

My own mother called me fat, even when I was not. I had such an on and off problem with eating disorders because I was never skinny enough for her. Even now, at the smallest weight I have ever been as an adult, she still tells me I am fat. But thank everything she does not get to me anymore, and I can treat my children differently. If she even slightly looks at my children the wrong way, she knows it is the biggest mistake she can make.

So much insecurity screamed out of me through all of this, all the attention, and all the harm I did to myself, my mind, and my body. I am not saying it is anyone's fault but my parents. This happened because I was a child. I cannot scream that enough. How could I know any better, or how to love myself, when no one around me loved me except in their own possessive, sick, abusive way? Who tells a child the sexual things he did? Who constantly belittles their child about their weight, personality, and everything else, and then says it is the child's fault because it is never the parents' problem? To my parents, they had no influence on what was done to us or what was shown to us, and by that statement I am speaking for myself and my siblings. Who, as an adult, leaves a man alone with their daughter knowing who he is?

The funny thing is that one of my mom's favorite sayings was that when I was with my kids' dad and he was extremely abusive and I would complain about him, she would say, "You knew who he was when you got with him." I remember finding out all the times he cheated, and I wanted to bond with my mom. I figured she would be there for her daughter after all the things she had been through. I told her and my dad that he cheated, and she said the same words, "You knew who he was when you got with him." She said that as if I knew he was going to continue to be horrible, or that I should not pray he would do better for himself and his family instead of staying stuck in the same abusive addictions. Do not think I am trying to be a saint here. I enjoyed my own dose of partying and problems too. But she still had the nerve to say that. Then my dad had the nerve to say that he took care of the house and the bills, and we had two babies together, that he was the father and I needed to get over it.

I was so mad. I was not supposed to be with him to begin with. We were young, we partied, and the easiest thing was to make a kid. He was also so great when we were young and dumb, and he even cheated before kids, but I was always taught to forgive things like that. I was so abused and groomed, and that carried into all relationships. I love my babies so much and I am thankful because they are why I am here today, but damn, making a kid was the easiest thing to do. In case some of you are as delusional as my mom, my dad, and others, kids come from sex. You can have sex with anyone, and sometimes, especially for women, you are not even sure you are doing it with the wrong partner. That is where babies come from, and that is not what makes you a parent. Being there, protecting, and caring for your child is what makes you a parent. Having a kid does not make you a mother or a father. Putting them before your own selfish, abusive needs is what makes you a parent, a good one.

I wanted to hurt my mom, and I remember whispering to her, "Well, he is not the only one that can do that." She slapped me with all her strength. My kids' dad even stepped in and asked what happened or what was said. I did not say anything, and neither did she. He kicked them out, and my dad apologized for her. I said, "She hit me," and he said he knew she was wrong. That is the type of bullshit he did. I honestly think that all the times she slapped me, my strong personality reminded her of him, and she was slapping me while thinking of him, because she would not dare do it to him. But that was the outrage she carried. She started fights multiple times and slapped hard like it was nothing, and it was just okay. One time I was so drunk she apologized the next day and I did not even remember it. Another time she slapped me so hard I pushed her. My little brother came down the stairs, saw it, and slapped the shit out of me. My mother had the nerve to thank him and start crying. That was her response and that was her reasoning. But it is funny coming from someone who allowed this kind of man to be alone with their daughter multiple times.

Back then, I knew so many people at school thought I looked like I was asking for it, like I was a slut. I know so many girls thought I was "weird," and truthfully, I probably was. I never had a middle ground. I already had a loud personality, but it seemed that whoever I got close to, my dad always made it seem negative, like I was negative. He shut people out of my life with negative comments about me, yet he was my best friend and he loved me so much. My mom did not help. I do not know if it was in her, but I was a fat child, then I lost the weight, then struggled on and off again. Hispanic mothers with abusers are often like that. You will never be good enough, and they criticize your body even if you look amazing, while they are out here looking like trail blazers.

But again, that is truly trauma. And if you finally stand up to them or say, "Look at you," there goes the excuse, "I already got my man, got married, and had kids," blah blah, sexist nonsense, so they think they have every right to criticize.

I see now why I ate. I eat my feelings, not knowing I was suppressing all of these things, not realizing I was being groomed. Rumors make you seem like the biggest slut possible, even when no one can prove they are true. That is what kids run with, rumors. Luckily, because of what I went through, I had the opposite reaction. I ran with those rumors and could not care less what other girls or guys thought of me. Even if they said things, I would fight, not because I cared, but because you would not be talking about it again. Most did not. They feared me, and the ones that did not, I made sure they did. I was a bully without realizing it, because I was bullied by my own family, my own people, because I was so "weird" from what I had been through and how I was raised. Kids were so mean to me from every direction, so I started fighting and shutting down. There was nothing you could do or say that was going to break me. There was nothing you could say that was more horrible than what I was already hearing from my parents or saying to myself. From what I had been through, I got to you before you got to me. But it took a long time before I started realizing I was hurting those who hurt me.

My mother's favorite thing to say was that I was a problem child, that I just fought to fight because I was a bad child, that there was no reason for my aggression, that I was just naturally a fighter and everything wrong was me, nothing to do with them whatsoever. They were never to be blamed, never the parents' fault.

Chapterfourteen

The Garage. This place was my hell from 13 to 17-ish years of age. It was his office/workspace, filled with cabinets in a row that turned into lined shelves where you could hide in between, do things you shouldn't be doing, and make it soundproof. The only thing you could hear sometimes was the vacuum going off when he cleaned his toner cartridges. Whenever I got called to this place, it honestly made me so fucking sad. I couldn't describe it. Even though I didn't exactly know anything he did was wrong, it felt like it just made me feel so bad. In that garage, so much happened, and until his arrest, I didn't even realize how blind, shame, and keeping it deep inside was wrong. One incident, before I was sexually active or even having sex, he went on to show me porn, but don't worry, it's not what you think. It was for educational purposes only. He was just showing his 14-year-old how to have sex, and how much pleasure you can get out of it, and how you please your man to keep them, and how enjoyable it is for a woman as well. Yes, these porn actresses showed me how real it was to get pleased and how. If you're thinking how fucking sick and demented, then good for you, because that's exactly right. That's sexual abuse. I was a CHILD, and that was his reasoning for showing it to me. Then he would get hard and say he had to adjust. It's natural to get horny from this. He was such a sick man. When I was in trouble, I would get put between the shelves, and to get out of trouble, I would have to give a long kiss or watch another porn for long lessons. A few times he showed me his penis to ask if he was too big. I bought a two piece once because I was so excited. I lost weight, and I wanted to wear a bikini like all the other 8th graders wore. My mom would never allow it, and she said my body made others lust over me, and I couldn't wear a two piece like the other girls because I had a much more sexual body, basically just not stick thin like the other girls. I always had thick thighs, flat stomach, and boobs, but I got it with her credit card anyways. My mom found out, gave it to my dad, and told him about it. Once again, I was called into the garage. I was scared. In front of her, he told me to put it on and to show it to him and come back into the garage. She allowed it, and I'm sure it wasn't what she thought it was going to be, but at this point, who knows. I put it on and then went into the garage. He asked me to walk and model it, and then he said yes, it's much too sexy. Boys will think I'm asking for it. Then he adjusted his pants like he got a boner over it. You put things back into your mind and never want to think about them again. He was my "protector," "my best friend." He would do anything for me, and why, to me, that was love, manipulation, lying, and getting my way. I lied so much, from where I was from to who my parents were, also cries for help, but people would catch on. Other kids and I was so focused on not caring about myself, I honestly didn't. It was not in my nature to fight everyone and do all the things I was taught. Belittle, lie, hurt, and apologize. Empty apologies was the very thing I learned from my dad. He would do all these horrible things, then pray on the Bible, put his hand on it, and be like, "I swear I will never touch you again." It leads to the time in the kitchen. He had a screwdriver and got mad I got in trouble at school for talking back, and he always used that saying, "I must not be a girl. I have balls," and no one was home, maybe my little brother was, but he stayed in his room and never left. And he chased me into the kitchen from the garage with a screwdriver, acting like he was going to check me for them. I was laughing at first, but this time he took the screwdriver and was hitting me with it between my legs. It hurt so bad I started crying. I said, "Why don't you do this to my brothers?" And I said, "Because you would look gay?" I don't even know why that sentence came out of my mouth. I was just tired of him attacking me like that and only me, and it's all I thought. I'm not even sure he didn't hurt my brothers. I know he did my older brother abusively, physical and mentally, but wasn't sure if he sexualized it, so I didn't think it was fair or the same. I felt like it was just me till later as an adult. I realized how much my brothers went through hell with that man as well. He stopped and said he was just playing. He didn't mean to hurt me or take it so seriously, that he loves me, and I was his girl, his love, his heart. He was a sick liar and abuser. He always promised on the Bible he wouldn't do things to me and then do them again. He justified it by going to church, then asking for forgiveness physically on the Bible by reading it, putting his hand on it, and asking for forgiveness. At one point, I told him to take the Bible and shove it up his ass, but it wasn't till years later. I was so fucking sick and tired of it. He went on to tell me he had sexual dreams about me. They were so real. He constantly got drunk and humiliated my mom with neighbors and getting drunk, but he didn't mean to. He was just drunk. Like I said, that was his get out of jail free card, and in our Mexican family, with tios, tias, cousins, anyone being drunk was valid in all crimes, sins, actions, and words.

I was in the 10th grade. I met a friend in high school, and we had so much fun with her. My parents would always let me stay the night at her place, even on school nights. I don't know if her parents knew something wasn't right in my home, just like the friends' parents in my younger days, but they always welcomed me with open arms and treated me like an extra daughter and let me stay there on school nights. It was amazing. I didn't think anything of it. My dad got me a car to help with my little brother, pick up and drop offs, and whatever else to get by on my own, and they didn't need to do much. One day I got invited to a party. It was a Sunday by a guy from work. I asked my friend if she wanted to go drinking and party with them. He had a friend. The party took place at a mansion in Plano, which wasn't far from Frisco, where we lived and attended school. They were not high schoolers and probably shouldn't have been hanging out with us. It wasn't really a party. It was more like two guys with alcohol, but it was fun. We drank so much. It was my first time and I think hers as well. We got wasted. She took off her top, very confident girl. I wasn't so confident back then and just with my body because of my parents, but she was beyond willing to show off, and all she did was take off her shirt, dancing around in her bra. I'm sure these guys were expecting more, and at this point, I have had sex and she hasn't, but I had only done it once with this guy, and he was so damn sweet about it, but we weren't boyfriend and girlfriend anymore. It was just honestly a great experience for me. Anyways, lol, we got so drunk we both occupied a bathroom and started vomiting, like exorcist type throwing up. The guys stopped wanting to do stuff with us. I would have too. It was bad. We couldn't stop for an hour. At one point, I stopped, and I knew she had play practice Sunday night because a big play was about to go off in school. She was one of the lead actresses, and she had to make it to practice. It was probably around 3, and we got wasted before then. I don't even think we drank that much. We just weren't used to drinking, and we didn't exactly have some beer. We went straight to the liquor. I told her we had to go, to stop throwing up and get in the car. I was still very drunk. I shouldn't have been driving. The guys honestly tried to stop us from driving, but we explained we had to get home because of our parents, and they stepped aside.

Chapter fifteen

We got to my house, and I don't know how I am truly surprised we didn't crash and kill ourselves and others. No one knew we were drinking, and back then, Mothers Against Drunk Drivers wasn't a thing, and we didn't really get talked to about drinking and driving. I didn't expect to drink, but it felt so nice, and during those times, there were light commercials and talks. It wasn't brought up like it is today, or did the law come down hard on it at the time. Watching your parents do it like it was natural or family, you just didn't think much of it. My dad came out of the house and knew we were wasted. He kept saying things. I don't remember much. I remember him getting in my car. My friend was in the passenger side, and I was in back, and he drove her home. She puked at her rehearsal. I don't know how or why she didn't smell, but she told me the next day they thought she just had a stomach bug and was able to stay home from school, and she got away with it because, of course, your normal parents aren't going to assume you're drinking at 15/16, at least not back then. Ignorance was bliss to the unblissful. When my dad was taking me back, he kept saying stuff about drinking and I shouldn't be driving and all the lectures in the world, and he checked my balance and held me up getting out of the car. I remember him taking me to my room and telling my family I was sick. He didn't even tell my mom I was drunk. I slept and slept. The next morning, he took me to school. He said I was begging him for sex when I was drunk and how attracted I was to him while drunk. I was sore everywhere. I felt so sick and told him to shut up. I did not say that. I didn't believe it for a second. I remember him staying in my room and seeing his figure, but I literally blacked out again, but I got so mad he said that. He always thought he was so much more than he was, so damn vain, and him saying I said that to him, I know I didn't. Even the "love" gestures made me sick, or how he would compliment me, and he was sitting there saying I wanted it. I was so broken by his accusations. Once again, I screamed, "SHUT UP." He didn't say anything else. That's where my Texas nurse at Centennial came in, the same Frisco High School that's been recently on the news. I was so disgusted by what he said, and I felt sore, so I went to the nurse. I lied and told her I went to a party and blacked out and wasn't sure what a guy did to me. She told me it was a privacy thing, and then she ended up calling my dad. He showed up and talked to the nurse. She said it's something that usually needs to go to the police. My dad just looked at her, then me, then he asked me if I think I was raped. I said I lied about it and I just wanted to go home. She allowed him to "handle it" and took me home. He asked if I ever said anything about him with how we "bond" or talk or anything at all. I told him I have never said anything about him, and it was about the party. He then says if I try to press charges on the guy, it would create a lot of problems. My mom would find out about the drinking, and it would keep me grounded for a very long time, and I would lose everything. I said it was fine, and I never said anything about it again. He started calming down and didn't bother me as much, except verbally abusive. He would give me anything I wanted financially from here on out, and I thought it was great, never thought anything bad again. He would still comment on my appearance. One day I was disgusting. The other day I was too sexy for my own good, but he was finally leaving me alone in a sense. He would make sexual comments to my friends once they were older and 18 or say humiliating things to me or about me and how I am nothing without a husband or boyfriend. Every time I did have a boyfriend, they were better than me, and I was lucky someone wanted me, his drunk nights, getting in fights with my brother, my mother, his embarrassing moments. He would drink till he pissed himself or started horrible name calling to anyone and everyone. It was pretty insane. Things like this continued. I started doing things like spending more than I should, hurt my siblings, get in fights, get drunk myself. He would tell me all these things, all the problems, all my mom's problems. He would always talk about her with no respect, and he hated her, so I had no respect for her, but that was years set up. My drinking was so bad. I partied, started fights, treated people badly, but still defended him, years and years of damage, forgetting and thinking he only did it to me because he thought we had a bond, never thought deeper than that to it or that he would ever harm anyone else.

Chapter sixteen

Years later, in between 17 and him being jailed, was just a mess of problems and trauma and alcoholism showing throughout my entire family. My dad had a drinking problem. I had one, and my older brother had one. The only "normal people" were my little brother and mom, and that's just meaning not drinking to the depths of darkness, making sure you forget you, your body, and your mind and keeping every dark secret darker. In my party days, in my life, even as a mother, I had nothing in control. I thought since my dad stopped and left me alone in the sexual sense, it was just hardship from him, and he was my best friend. He was always there for me financially and could call him for anything. I truly felt like it was my job to protect him and honor him, and that's how deep and sick it gets with grooming. You watch Law and Order SVU, one of my favorite shows as a kid and till this day, probably because I always knew something was wrong but never got the justice like in the show. Even watching it in front of my face, I didn't see it. If you have watched, most of the time, or someone with a healed, normal mind couldn't understand why these men and women defend their rapist and molesters, especially in the family, with all their heart, talking about them in such a high glory, but that's what grooming does. Some stranger raping or molesting a stranger, it's much easier to come out because you're not being taught to protect the person. Doesn't mean that's always the case, but in my case, it's family. In grooming cases, it's a close friend of the family, married in, church figure, or direct blood family. That's the difference why a lot of family think they can get away with the sick jokes, racism, sexual banter, bashing someone's life in general, and write it off as "we are family," but especially in these circumstances. In such a young age, something so heinous gets done young, you don't see the difference between right or wrong. You're stunted in what you know and what happened at such a young age, not understanding your mind or body or the feelings you feel, and in your family, the only people you have known to love or trust are the very ones turning the other cheek because, again, "family loyalty and bond." I saw some of my dad's sisters saying and doing disgusting things, how they treated their own children, prioritizing the drink or disgusting acts, being inappropriate themselves, and everyone brushing it along as if you don't know anything else, and you have everyone you love and that should be protecting you also supporting this person, and that's abuse from the whole damn nest. That's what enablers of the groomer do. When I tell you there's not just one monster in stories like these, that's why. It's not just the person doing it. It's also the family telling you to ignore it and supporting the very person causing the damage. Even if it's not family directly, someone holding a financial situation against you is the same thing. It is abuse. Someone telling you not to say something because they pay the bills or will give money or you can't survive financially without them or offer to buy you something, pay for something, that's abuse. An abuser would do that, and even if not directly from the person abusing you, if someone is telling you to cover because they take care of you or them, that's just as disgusting and enabling abuse, so you might as well be doing it yourself. Sick enough to do this to another friend or adult, but to do this to your own children is beyond despicable.

You may not have sat there and watched, but not protecting, not defending, and finding a way to keep it a secret when someone comes to you for help makes you just as much to blame. Don't give a damn what you prove in court. More people need to be held accountable for these actions and abuse, and thank goodness they are. Even the law is changing, evolving, and charging people.

Witnessing my brother drinking himself to death because of his own abuse and trauma was devastating. Sadly, some of it wasn't even my dad's doing. A church man came into his life and began that troubled journey of hell for him. That part is not my story to tell, but what I can say again is this: how does a parent allow a grown man to take your son for weeks? I don't give a damn if Peter came back from the dead, you just don't allow certain things unless you're asking for heartache or setting your children up for failure at such a young age, making them feel like they can't even understand how to stand up for themselves or know anything about themselves.

The church member ended up killing himself right around the time my brother broke down to the point that drinking consumed him and he wasn't himself anymore. My dad told me he confessed some things about being abused, and I asked why he wasn't doing anything about it. He said it was done with now, so what could he do? Looking back, with everything that's happened, it's so dark, but maybe he always knew about it and didn't care or even gained from it. He also said others were coming forward to speak against this person and they wanted him involved. Instead of recognizing what was done to my brother was wrong and sick, my dad basically told him to get over it.

What my brother went through and how he was told to handle it was absolutely wrong and deeply disturbing. That's just my perspective on it, with everything and how my dad handled things. I wouldn't be surprised if this was intentional. My brother was so smart, so athletic, yet he just shut down. As kids, my little brother and I didn't understand his anger. We thought he was just trying to fight my dad over his drinking, and we assumed he was being a loser because that's what my dad said, a coward, a girl, someone who couldn't handle it. He hurt him for being hurt.

He was just a child, and the ones who failed him were my parents. They gave him no chance to be normal, healthy, or get the help he needed. To this day, family thinks he's just a loser, even though he tries everything to be the son my dad would accept. Now that my dad is in jail, he acts like my brother is the most amazing son for standing by him, but again, grooming does that. My brother seeks the acceptance and love he never received, never growing from what happened to him mentally and physically, who could?

Chapter seventeen

Before all that happened to him, my dad abused him physically and emotionally, emasculating him and making sure we all thought the same. Even in jail, my mom enables my dad to this day and keeps my brother within reach, so we all think so poorly of him, as if it's all his fault. But now, getting sober and knowing what I know, I don't blame him one bit. I blame his parents for never giving him a chance. They took his innocence, his humanity, and any sense of maturity, leaving him stuck where he was. I love him dearly, but because he's not in a place of healing, he remains trapped in our family's past.

He beat my little brother constantly while growing up and was exceptionally cruel to us. We couldn't understand; we thought he was psycho and absolutely ridiculous. My little brother lived a very different life from us and was shielded from so much, yet I always defended him against our older brother and even got my own ass kicked for it. Now I can see what was wrong. It was pure jealousy, a child thinking, why him? He thought he was alone in his suffering. We didn't know, as kids, about the abuse, hatred, or misunderstanding in our home. How could a child know when that's all they have ever known?

It's insane how much we normalized traumatic homes, mainly because we didn't compare or talk about it. Back then, you didn't get involved with other families because you didn't want your own dirty laundry aired. Everything was about appearances. And it's still like that, Facebook pictures, family posts, "greatest mom and dad," and then arrests happen, and all the dirty details come out.

So many murderers were considered amazing husbands and friends. There's no way it was the mother, she was always seen as amazing. People could claim he follows God and would never do something like this because they only knew the lie. Even women proudly post about men who do nothing for them, claiming they are the best thing because they made a kid with them. Trauma. It takes far more than sex and creating a child to be a good parent or partner.

The number of people who bashed me or reached out after my dad's arrest or saw him on the news were in complete shock. From my trauma and grooming, if I hadn't seen it myself, I wouldn't have believed he did that. I thought my life was unfair, like my older brother. There was no way to realize at a young age that it was wrong, or that we weren't the only ones experiencing it. We were in the same hell, in the same house but where could you turn?

He would take knives, scream, and threaten to hurt us. I now see he wasn't a bad kid, he was hurting and didn't know how to handle it. No child would! Trauma like this shapes a child into an adult who doesn't know how to cope. Hurt people hurt or heal, but what chance do you have not to turn to drugs or alcohol when you can't understand your feelings? Relationships turn toxic, and abuse perpetuates abuse.

I'm not excusing hurting anyone. If you choose to continue the toxic behavior, you've decided not to get help, and at some point, it becomes pure evil. Some people may never regret it. Some are far gone in their ignorance and cruelty, taking it to their graves, and you have to accept that. Healing and doing better is something we must do for ourselves.

My poor brother stays trapped in the past. Mom and dad do no wrong. My little brother's success isn't earned, it was given. And I'm still the lying little girl who supposedly caused him to be abused. He is hurting, and when you can't channel that hurt, it turns into anger. That sick cycle continues. People exploit others' trauma for personal gain, pretending to love them while showing everyone else they are nothing.

Narcissists thrive on their victims, and growing up, it was always us against the world.

We fought, lied, and struggled to survive. My older brother had rage issues. If we had proof and talked about everything, the truth might have come out. But that can never happen. Mom and dad keep us at each other's throats, in the dark, so the truth never surfaces. They are the victims, and we supposedly did this to them. My dad is in jail because of me, and that's all my family will ever see.

Years later, at 26 with two kids, I had a best friend. I trusted her with my heart and soul about motherhood, my family, my boyfriend, and the kids' father. We were both unhealthy, feeding off our toxic traits. She shared her friends' secrets and demeaned everyone, yet I was a fool not to see she did the same. Biggest red flag: she hated dogs. Everyone has their quirks, but hating dogs is a universal warning. The point is not her, it's my dad and the constant disgust and destruction he created. One day she was running late, and I was babysitting her kids. My dad called, and I answered.

All I heard was my friend's voice. I thought he was calling to explain why she was running late, but it was an accidental dial. They were talking. She was saying some sexual things, and so was he. She brought up needing money, and he mentioned that she knew what he had to do. I was in her home with the kids, and he was at our home where my mother still lived, probably at work, because in his twisted version of being Hispanic, she stayed a housewife at this point. She had to work just as hard for money and bills, but he was still the man and got to do whatever he wanted. He believed in a corrupt, old Mexican version of marriage, but only when it fit his narrative. She still had to take care of him, even financially, and to her, in the fucked up, twisted loyalty of the marriage she committed to and was blinded by. Meanwhile, he was doing that with my friend behind her back, in her home.

I hung up the phone and texted him, "Are you fucking serious?" She came and picked up the kids, and we didn't talk about it. Then my dad, when I got home, was in his "office" and just started laughing. He said he couldn't believe he was stupid enough to butt dial me. He admitted he had been having a thing with my friend for a while now, and they had been doing it here, in his car, etc. Once again, my mother didn't do anything for him, and it was her fault that he did that. He deserved to be happy too, blah blah, the same bullshit with him. He said he was so thankful he had a best friend like me, that I was grown enough to understand and just keep it to myself.

Honestly, I thought about telling my mom a few times. I wanted to yell at my brother after court when he said he believed my dad, but what was the point? This is the type of shit he has done our whole lives. All the secrets, making sure we didn't understand how wrong it was, blaming my mother and saying she was the narcissist. Maybe she was wrong too for all the past stuff, but it is important to understand that the same hell we were living, she was living too, from her past and from him. You had no other option but to defend him. The only family she had supported that, and in their eyes, as a "husband under God," that is all she has ever known. This type of trauma and abuse gets recycled and repeated.

But you get a choice in your life, especially when it comes to your kids. I can never be okay with it or fully understand it, but it is not for me to understand. It is for me to do what is right for me, to advocate for my children, and to make sure they never go through what I went through by healing. I can't be the same child carrying the weight of an adult and their past trauma and abuse, and I sure can't let my children do the same. It was getting there, and I did what I had to do. Unfortunately, it wasn't until he was arrested, and I started counseling and AA, that helped me face my trauma and past in a healthy way and be able to come forward.

Chaptereighteen

I moved to Anna, Texas, with my kids' dad and the kids, all three of them. Both my brothers moved in with us. I always felt like I owed them for being such a bad kid and for wanting to mother them. My brother had just gotten out of a coma from drinking himself practically to death, and from what I have written and shared, we can all understand why. When you have dark secrets, you want to black them out, and that is what alcohol does. It is a temporary fix for trauma.

This was before we got our home in Anna. We got it a few months after he woke up from the coma, but they never thought he was going to wake up. He was bleeding from everywhere and had failing organs. My mom never stopped crying and praying. At one point, she screamed at me about something, not in a bad way, but out of devastation. She loved my brother in the best way she could after everything.

I remember going to visit my brother. My parents told me where he was, and when I went, he was in the ICU. I had moved out of my parents' house a while ago and hadn't seen my brother in a long time. I had to take in his dog because my dad wouldn't allow him to have him. When I got to the hospital, I went to the ICU. It was a lot for me. I was so sad seeing people that sick. They told me the room number and opened the door for me.

I walked in, and the man in the bed looked like bones, like an older man who hadn't eaten. I was relieved and told the nurse, "Oh my God, this isn't my brother. You must have the wrong person." She turned to the chart, said his full name clearly, and then said, "This is him, hun." I looked back over. He was in a coma, with a tube out of his mouth and many other places. I just cried, bawled actually. I wanted to know why he felt so bad about himself that he did this, why he tried to kill himself without a gun, why he hated himself.

Overwhelming sadness and guilt swept over me. I should have been there more, talking to him more. There was obviously something wrong. I told him I loved him so much, and that if he was tired of fighting, I understood, but that he could get better. We were told it wasn't promising, but only time would tell.

As I was leaving, my dad showed up. He was so drunk. I said, "Do you not understand that's what got him here?" You have no sympathy, no remorse. He told me to shut the fuck up and said it honestly would be a relief if my brother died. He said my brother was so much trouble and a burden on our family, and that here was another thing he was taking from everyone. That was the first time I truly saw evil, not from anything he did to me, but from what he said about my brother. He did not realize it was all his fault, but those were his words in that moment.

My brother ended up waking up a few months later, but he had a lot to get through, and he had to stay sober. The nurse was kind of bitchy about it, or maybe just more realistic, because we all know with alcoholism and addiction, even after life threatening situations, how easy it is to go back rather than face sobriety. She said it was more likely he would drink again than not.

He needed a place to stay, and my parents said no, that it was my responsibility. He could barely walk, and I had just had my third baby. She always made him happy. When he first woke up, he wanted her in his arms, even though he couldn't speak yet or make sounds. He could barely hold her without assistance. He always said his bubbles saved him.

He stayed sober for a long time and recovered so well. He followed through, even when they said he would require a transplant. He deserved to live, but with all that trauma and abuse still living in memory, it is hard to live. He is doing it at his own pace and for his own reasons. It is not my job to worry about it, but I did care for him in any way I could.

Chapter nineteen

We stayed at the Anna house for a good amount of time, drinking excessively and showing a lack of responsibility. My dad and mom were "splitting up," so she would stay with us sometimes but had moved into an apartment with him. He claimed to have a girlfriend or several. My friend might have still been one, I didn't know or care but I did know about the other one I found out about after the arrest. She couldn't believe it. Imagine that.

We had a party one night, and he got obliterated, as he always did. He would always drive home drunk from Anna, Texas, to Allen, Texas, even if we tried to stop him. Even with everything my older brother was going through, he tried to run him over once for trying to stop him from leaving. He could be inappropriate with my friends, and they would always say it was okay after I apologized and asked him to stop. He always got mad if I tried to tell him to drink water, stop drinking, or not be inappropriate with my friends. They would always get uncomfortable, but it was always me. I was being lame and a loser and didn't know how to party.

That went on for a while, even with children around. Fun was so important, and my partner didn't drink anywhere near the way I did. I thought I deserved it. I was that mother at the time, because I gave birth to them and believed I was owed all the sympathy and fun. At this point, my ex had been involved in so many cheating scandals that I just had to get over them. I would drink and then let my real feelings come out with the alcohol. It was so dysfunctional, I can't even imagine how awful it must have looked to anyone on the outside. But we were always the ones in the right; everyone else was wrong, and we were doing just fine.

My dad always found a way to fix it or babysit to help me mentally, but it was more like everything I knew he never wanted it coming out. He came over just to drink and constantly talk badly about my mother, never taking accountability for anything he had ever done or created. It was always someone else's fault. The same applied to his family. The amount of lies he fed them about always helping and everything being on him, claiming his entire family were losers and that we did nothing for him, was astounding. He would borrow money from his sisters and feed them a fabricated story so it was always "poor him" for dealing with all of us and "what a good man" for putting up with it, and that he shouldn't have to. He scammed in life, work, and anything else he could. I don't blame them for believing him. He was the ultimate manipulator and narcissist. He abused anyone who ever cared for or loved him, including his sisters, who defended him to this day. Family was everything, and that's all they were taught, even to defend the sick and twisted. What could you do differently when you're always taught that loyalty to family comes above all, even above morality?

* * *

The night of the arrest: my friend of so many years came over that night with her daughter and another friend. We wanted to go out to celebrate something, it could have been her friend's birthday. My kids' dad came with us, since we were still together at the time. Her daughter called my dad "Gampy," like my kids did. She was basically my sister, all we had ever known. I was there the day her daughter was born. We had been friends since we were sixteen, and to me, they were my family.

In all the craziness, it's still hard to believe, because when she was in difficult situations, my dad always helped her but who knows how much of that was manipulated for her. Before her daughter was even born, he would talk about her looks and beauty and say that if he ever divorced my mom, he would go after her. It's no wonder my mom was always uncomfortable, but I didn't see it that way. I couldn't, I was always pitted against her, and he had a reasoning for all his actions. I called her daughter my niece and loved her dearly. I was there when she was born, and during this particular night, regardless of what the articles and news said, she was five years old, my son was six, and my daughters were four and three.

We went out celebrating something in September, it could have been her friend's birthday. My dad offered to watch the kids. He was a regular babysitter. That's the thing about him: when I had my kids, he was always there for me, more than my mom. She always made sure I was the woman, the mother, and my kids' dad and significant other deserved all the help, never having to be responsible for the kids because that was "not their job." Being a father when he paid the bills was out of the question, even though my dad really did pay the bills. It was the most twisted reasoning or way of life ever.

He always helped, though, at every appointment, every time I needed a break, anything the kids needed, he always got it: diapers, clothes, whatever. He was the most hands-on Gampy ever. People were jealous, saying what a good dad and grandpa he was, even friends of mine. I was just so blessed, but they never knew what it took to get there. The biggest lesson: don't ever envy anyone.

It never crossed my mind that my children might not be safe, because he was my dad and the way he loved those babies and acted around them was genuine. It was just a "me thing," and he was going through his own issues sometimes. Honestly, my past never crossed my mind again until his arrest, because the dad and Gampy he was after I had my first, and then the two after that, he was the most hands-on, caring dad and Gampy. He had watched all the kids before and agreed to watch them so we could go out. He would never get drunk when he watched the kids; it was an unspoken rule. At the time, he always watched them with my mother at home until we moved, and he had watched them a few times prior during the day, doing a good job.

My children and her child adored my dad. They got so excited when he came over or when they saw him. I'm telling you, this is how it's set up: when people speak on his behalf, they wouldn't even consider the inappropriate comments he made to my friends about their looks and "jokes" about dating. We didn't realize that it didn't stop there. It's not about her being an adult; it's that line of not knowing where it's going to go from there, or if you have no reason to cross it but do anyway. I'm not saying every sin is the same, or that any person pushing a boundary would hurt a child. It's the fact that we didn't see past that, or I didn't. I thought it was a "me thing" and our so-called "bond," as he constantly put it, especially after seeing him with my children. I never saw a danger.

If you don't understand, especially with trauma, grooming, and abuse, you can't help but think, "how stupid," or many other things. But if you have been through it and are healing, or have a past of it, you can see how much you relate to it, it slowly clicks. It's scary and sad, and explains why so many people can't say anything; they get tricked into thinking "never him." He drank to death at any other time, but he was good around the kids.

We had a bottle of scotch on top of the fridge. We asked him not to drink it until we got back, and he could take it with him. It was brand new and gifted from a friend. He agreed. Both my brothers were living with me in my home. Both slept nights and were up during the day. We left kind of late. I saw my older brother before we left; he was always trying to bond with my dad somehow, even if it meant belittling himself or enduring my dad's constant teasing. It was "playing," but he participated for a bit before we left.

We made sure my three kids were asleep, and my friend got her daughter to sleep in the front living room on a pallet of blankets, where she was going to sleep when we got back. We wanted them in bed before we left to make it easier for my dad to just sit back, instead of dealing with little ones running around, since he was already doing us the favor by watching them.

We drove to the Allen outlets and enjoyed some drinks at Kelly's at the Village. We got bored, it was a weekday, and it wasn't as lively as usual, so we decided to make a final stop at Applebee's. I checked on my dad a few times to make sure the kids were okay, and he sent normal text messages back saying it was fine. We mentioned we were making one more stop.

At Applebee's, we just sat back, drank, and talked. The girls were taking shots. My kids' dad decided to step back on drinking since he was driving home and had learned his lesson from the past. He had a beer or two at the last place, nothing more. My friend and her friend were staying the night and not driving, so they were having a good time.

I got a couple of messages from my dad while at Applebee's, and they didn't make sense. I got worried and went to the restroom to call him. I made the call in the stall, and he couldn't even speak; he was completely slurring his words. My first thought was, "Oh shit." I was super worried about the kids. He was with my baby, he could drop her if she woke up or fall on one of the kids. He was a terrible drunk, and he was drunk. He even yelled at me saying he was drunk. I sent him text messages, pissed off that he got that wasted with the kids.

I walked out of the restroom and said we had to leave immediately because my dad was wasted. The girls laughed, didn't think much of it,

and took their time finishing their drinks. I calmed down too, realizing we would be home soon enough. They finished, paid the tab, which took forever, and then we headed home.

Chapter twenty

When we got home, the garage was left open, and we thought it was strange. We always closed it, so maybe someone exited through the garage instead of the front door. We pulled in. My kids' father either went in first or second, which made me first or second. I do not remember the exact order, but I remember entering through the garage into the hallway. From the garage door, the hallway leads directly in front of the stairs, and to the far right there is an opening into the front living room, where my friend's little one had been sleeping, but she was not asleep.

She stood straight up from lying down, and my dad was on his knees or kneeling and then to the right. He kind of rolled down. My friend and her friend were right behind me. We asked what was happening. Everything felt strange, and it felt wrong instantly, like something was not okay. The little one being awake like that was alarming. She shot up and looked sad or scared but did not fully get up. She lifted herself using her arms, as if she had been lying on her back with her legs still down.

My kids' dad knew something was wrong, and he ran away to our room. He just left us there, even though he knew something was going on, because we started asking the little one what was wrong. Then we saw that my dad had her shorts and panties in his hand. My kids' dad ran away, listening to all the commotion, and did not want to get involved. He left three women to handle the situation. That is his character. He is a little bitch. You might think that is harsh, but anyone who chooses anything over the protection of his child or children deserves that description. This does not just have to do with that night, but that was when I first realized it. Things between us went downhill from there. I think that was the moment I realized I never did or could love someone like that. This event and the trauma that followed got in the way of ever letting ignorance blind me again to the idea of a "happy home" or love.

The little one's mom then asked her to get up, and that is when we realized she did not have her panties or shorts on. She then asked my dad why he had her shorts and panties in his hand again. He could not even make out his words. He was slurring so badly. We brought the little one into the restroom after we got her clothes. I asked her gently and told her not to be scared, that she was not in trouble, but asked if Gampy had done something to her. She said that he licked her "no no," referring to her vagina.

I knew she was telling the truth. She was too little to know to say something like that, and she loved her Gampy so much and trusted him. The little one's mom started crying and asked me what she should do. Instantly, I said, "Call the cops." Because of her past, and I am sure having been forced to sweep her own family's disgusting secrets or actions under the rug, like always, Hispanic family loyalty even against sick crimes because the cultural corruption cycle continues, I said yes, strongly and firmly, to call the cops.

She started calling them but was having a hard time getting the words out because she was crying, so I grabbed the phone from her. We kept the little one in the bathroom. I took the phone and started explaining, but the 911 operator kept asking questions. I yelled to send the cops to the address I gave her now, that we needed help immediately. Something along those lines. I feel bad now, because I know the operator was just doing her job, but the questions felt like nonsense and like wasted time.

I panicked. I acted strong and knew it was the right thing to do, but at the same time I could not believe this was happening, that we caught him doing this, and that we trusted him with the kids. My friend's friend started helping me get my dad into the kitchen and away from us. He was slurring things like, "Are you serious? You are going to regret this. You are so fucking ungrateful." Her friend pushed him further into the kitchen and told him to shut the hell up. He was too drunk to fight or protest. Out of anger, she hit him a couple of times and even kicked him. She was angry and disgusted, and she had every right to be.

The Anna Police Department arrived. The police officer took me outside and asked me what happened, and I explained. Then they brought my dad out and arrested him. I cried and said, "How could you do this?" He called me a bitch and said I did this to him, that he should have never babysat for me, that I was ungrateful, and that it was my fault. That was as far as the conversation went, and it was the last time I saw him in person until court. The officer overheard and told him to shut up because of the felony and crime he was being charged with, and because of her age. The Texas Rangers showed up.

Police, fancy police that handle child sex crimes like this, like SVU. They came in black cowboy hats, all black, fancy SUVs, several of them. They took each of us into separate vehicles and interviewed us. They interviewed the little one and possibly my kids. I cannot remember every detail. That lasted for hours. My kids woke up. They did not see my dad get arrested. The cops and Texas Rangers were so kind to them. They were dancing around with the little one because they were children and innocent. Thank all the light for their resilience. They did not understand how bad the crime was that had been committed. She was not physically hurting.

Regardless of what witnesses later wanted to claim in my home, saying she was dancing and happy, of course she was. She is a child. She saw her "cousins" being spoken to kindly. They did not make it scary for her. None of us did. She had already been through something no one should have to experience, especially a child. But because she was happy, some people wanted to claim nothing happened. That is what grooming does. That is what abuse does. Do you really think you should defend the abuser and look for reasons they are innocent? If I had not witnessed it myself, believe me, as scary as it is, I would have questioned it too.

They woke my brothers up to interview them, but they said they did not hear or see anything. I called my mother. I blew up her phone until she woke up. When she finally answered, she was angry. I told her what happened, and she responded with, "What do you want me to do about it?" as if she did not care, or as if I was wrong for even bothering her. She hung up.

Chapter twenty-one

They told us we did not have time and had to go straight to the hospital. My kids' dad finally appeared and watched my little ones. I went with my friend and her daughter to Children's Hospital to do a sexual assault kit. I was a zombie, but I was there for my friend and her daughter. When I got home, the sun was up. I got a call saying that the kids and I had to go to a place in Plano for the children to be interviewed by a detective and Child Protective Services, who handle these types of crimes and situations.

We got one hour of sleep and were told we needed to come in and bring the children and everyone who had been there to be interviewed. When we arrived, my friend and her little one were already there. My phone was flooded with texts. It was on the news, social media, everywhere. The Anna Police Department released a statement after being asked not to, because it involved a young child, but they did it anyway.

They interviewed my son. Being six, he was able to share the most. He said Gampy never did anything to him, and the interviewer confirmed she did not believe Gampy ever harmed my children. It made me cry uncontrollably. I could not understand it, and again it felt unreal. All that ran through my head was, he is ruining lives, for what? One of the Texas Ranger detectives met us at the interview location. I told him it was on the news and that I had been getting nonstop calls. He apologized and said that was not supposed to happen. He asked if I wanted him to do something about it. I said no. I told him that if it were any other person, releasing the information to warn the public would be the right thing to do, to help protect people and encourage victims to seek justice. Why would it be wrong now? Because it was my dad this time?

We finally got home. I took a nap, and then the doorbell started ringing. News vans showed up. It was nonstop for hours, waiting outside. Friends came to check in, neighbors too. It was an absolute nightmare. There was genuine concern and love from some people. They brought food, care packages, and kindness. I sat in the living room, kneeling on the floor, watching the news, seeing his face repeatedly on the TV, crying.

My little brother came downstairs at one point. He was never one to show emotion. He sat next to me and hugged me. He said he knew how hard it was for me to do this, or something close to that. It was sweet, caring, and sympathetic. I remember being shocked by it. He continued hugging me, then got up and left.

I sat there trying to make sense of the situation. It felt like a nightmare, except you knew you were awake. The confusion of how this could be real was overwhelming. I felt numb but still felt everything. It was the feeling you get when something terrible has happened, but you cannot believe it and do not want to. That is exactly what it felt like, babbling, repetitive, pure insanity. I listened to the news replay the story over and over, full of truths and lies. It would not be the news without both.

There was a ringing sound, and I was in a trance, wondering what it was. Was it the TV? Was it in my head? I realized it was the doorbell. I got up off the floor, not realizing how long I had been sitting there, but long enough for my body to hurt. As I walked to the door, I felt nervous about who might be there. My mother? No way. It had been over 24 hours since I called her, and there had been no contact. Not a single word. Even after I told her what was happening, she acted like she did not care, like I was bothering her.

I wondered who else might recognize me, my last name, or his face from the news, and my connection to it.

I opened the door without thinking. Bright flashing lights and microphones filled my vision. Reporters yelled the same questions over and over.

"Was it your daughter?"

"Did you know?"

C h a p t e r t w e n t y-t w o

After the Damage

We all go through difficult moments, wondering if we can breathe, if we can make it. Is it going to get better? Because it sure in hell doesn't feel like it is. I remember so vividly lying on the floor, wondering how I could go on. I wasn't even the actual state's victim, but that's the problem with these cases and these people who hurt their victims. It's never just one. They don't understand how many people it hurts, and how many monsters and victims emerge from these situations.

If you're lucky and by lucky, I mean lottery-winner lucky, like winning over $1,000 on a $1.00 scratch-off, you will get supportive family and friends. The court will rule in your favor, there will be only one monster in your case, justice will be served, and those around you will help you heal and learn to love not only yourself, but also the support that surrounds you.

Unfortunately, that's not usually the case. By not usually, I mean statistically, it's far more likely that this will not happen. I'm not trying to bring out the negative; I'm just being honest. This account is just that, the honest, true, horrifyingly real experiences but it's also meant to help those who are suffering realize that they are not alone.

Regardless of your case, even if you are in the middle of a court battle or debating whether to tell anyone, those battles are not for the weak. This is what this chapter is about, because in real cases, silent or loud, in real situations, whether in your mind or on a court document, when your name is listed as the victim, there is often more than one monster. It could be family telling you to sweep it under the rug. It could be people telling you that you're lying or that no one will believe you because of how charming the abuser is, or because of what others will lose if your truths are revealed. No matter the situation, those are monsters too.

This is more about what happens outside the heinous crime itself. That's what this entire chapter is about: justice. But we are not talking solely about the legal sense of it. I mean, we are, but we are not. This account is about all of it: the damage, the family, the before and after, everything that is caused both through the court system and outside of it, in your mind and at home.

I want whoever is reading this to either understand or want to understand. I want every single person to fight for themselves, because no one deserves to be hurt by a stranger or a loved one, or by someone who was supposed to protect us. I will never understand the concept of people using "I love you" as a form of abuse or manipulation. That's what I had to deal with throughout this ordeal. I couldn't believe it was happening, but the worst part was the lack of support, being called a liar and having to stay strong.

It was strangers, not family, who offered me the utmost support, and I am forever thankful for that. But the very people who lived through this with me wanted to believe him. It got to the point where my own mother didn't speak to me, and I think that was the worst. Instead of siding with a child or even my own children and what we had to endure, she supported the very man she claimed she was "finally going to divorce," as if she didn't know his abusive behavior personally. Even if it was just for herself to fight for, everything could have come together, but it didn't. She even got my brothers to turn against me and support my father.

I can't even imagine, given the threats his sisters made against me and the children, what she had to deal with regarding them. But that wasn't my problem. And as I've said, that's what an abuser does. He knows exactly how to manipulate, and he never targets someone who would challenge him. He goes for the quiet, the easily directed. But what a shame. The moment you find your voice, you don't just have to confront the person who committed the crime, the abuser, but also the people who support the abuser and shame you for doing the right thing.

"What happened here?"

All from different news stations, wanting more information than the small amount the Anna Police Department had leaked for their fifteen minutes of fame. I do not fully blame them. I understand wanting to warn the public. I usually admire it and feel grateful when it protects children and others. But that day, it was not protecting us. It was hurting us over something horrific that someone else did.

My dad.

Chapter twenty-three

From the crime itself in September 2019 to court in March 2021, it was two very long, hard years. I experienced loss of family and friendships. Little One's mother always tried to stay my friend, but I'm sure it was difficult for her to navigate everything while dealing with the court proceedings.

A number of my father's sisters called, some were supportive, but only one. The rest accused me of lying, claiming none of it was true. My brothers returned to live with my mother, and somehow, I was also considered to be lying. My older brother started talking to my father and claimed he was innocent. My brother supported the same narrative, and somehow, all our lives were destroyed for reasons we didn't understand. There was no way my father, or I, was doing this for personal gain or to avoid repaying him for financial help.

Yes, some crazy things were being said that put me in the worst position of my life, mentally, financially, and physically. I was even hospitalized when this first happened in McKinney. I told the staff what was going on, and I felt like I was having a heart attack. They admitted me, hid my identity, medicated me, and let me rest. They prescribed me Xanax, which I took once, falling asleep for four hours. I understood the purpose and it helped, but I flushed the medication because I couldn't properly care for my children while under its effects.

We moved from the home in Anna to a less-than-ideal place, but it was away from everything. Even after the hospital, handling everything naturally was incredibly hard. I couldn't drink anymore because it triggered severe panic attacks. I turned to weed, which helped me stay calm, laugh again, and eat properly. I used it recreationally, and it truly helped me maintain balance.

I started working as a bartender and met my best friend and soul sister, one of the best things to come out of this tragic ordeal. I always tried to maintain communication with Little One and my friend, despite the hate from their families and mine. There was never a time I didn't love them dearly. The reason I fought so hard was for justice, for Little One, for myself, and for my family, even if they didn't want it.

When everything first happened and he was arrested, my family supported me for about fifteen minutes before turning against me. This happens more often than not. That's why I always prepare for every possible outcome. In these situations, the damage doesn't come only from the predator or abuser. There are many monsters in these cases.

I was blessed that the Collin County District Attorney's office did an amazing job. They helped me every step of the way, showed kindness to my children, and demonstrated true compassion for this type of situation. Their goal is to put away the individuals who harm children, and their number one priority is justice for these kids who have experienced trauma that should never have happened.

I wish someone had fought this hard for me or my brothers. Things could have been very different. You never realize how these experiences can ruin lives and permanently alter a child. Even with justice, the mental support you need is immense. I mean it when I say, even if everything goes right in court, even with a strong support system and parents backing you, it helps tremendously but how does a child comprehend what happened to them? How do they understand the reasoning behind it? It is both a physical and mental beatdown, no matter what.

I started drinking again, and it kept getting worse every time I got an email saying court was happening. Then I would get another email a few days before the court date saying it was rescheduled. This went on and off for almost two years. I didn't talk to my mom or brother for almost half a year. She never brought up my dad, but she started getting comfortable letting my kids talk to him and video chat with him in jail. They told my children he was in a submarine. I wish I didn't allow it and that I had been in a better place to stop it. I brought it up once while drunk, and she blew me off.

Then slowly my older brother felt comfortable talking to me and asking why I did this, saying my dad was innocent, and even saying the little girl was smiling, laughing, and playing that night. How could he have done what he did if she was doing all that? I remember yelling at him that she was a CHILD, a kid. What did you expect her to do or how did you expect her to react? She was so little and innocent and saw my dad as her gampy. She couldn't even realize how wrong it was. My dad manipulated my brother. He always wanted my dad's love, and my dad was always disappointed in my older brother, never good enough. But with this, he was able to redeem himself and be in good standing with the father he always wanted. That is what grooming does.

Again, regardless, the abuse, emotional and physical, and the belittling, that's how they keep their victims continuing the hurt. This is what narcissists do. He told my brother what a great son he is, that family stands by his side. I don't know my little brother's take on it or why he holds on. He lived very differently from us, but that could be my mother. He loves her dearly. She protected him enough from my dad and from us, so she was always "mother the great," and she could do no wrong.

Poor kid has no idea what she does and how she pits us against each other, or keeps negative stories or lies about my older brother and me. My little brother is perfect, and she vents to him about all the problems we cause, even if we don't anymore, even if we help her. That will never be the story, or the truth can never be told. She turned into the very pain she lived, just like my dad. She made sure to paint herself as the savior to us. As a mother, she's amazing and such a great mom, and she must be a saint to deal with me and my older brother. We would never be as good as much. We are mistakes, and my little brother is everything she always dreamed of in a child. That is why my big brother has such resentment toward him, and sadly, how much resentment my little brother has toward us.

Don't get me wrong, when we were younger, we did a lot of messed up things. But we were so young ourselves. We also did a lot of messed up things as adults because of what happened to us and all we ever learned. We learned to hurt, mess up, and use everything we learned in our toxic upbringing against each other. No matter how we hurt each other, we were told you have to get over it because we are family. That's not how it works or how you treat any human being, not family, not friends, not anyone. But it's what we did and what we've been through.

Hopefully someday he understands all this. There is a time when you learn from your trauma and become better than what you've been through, or you repeat the same experiences by hurting those who hurt you. Sadly, that's what often ends up happening. I am learning so much from all this, but I sought the help I needed through counseling, my sponsor, and getting sober. I was using drinking as a crutch to get over the trauma and experiences at the time, and it did nothing of the sort. It made my problems bigger or just pushed them out of sight and mind until I came back from my blackout therapy.

My brother is being enabled by his own unresolved hurt, and he stays in the same character defects. He will never get what he needs to move on and heal until he figures it out for himself and gets help. But his story is not mine to finish for him. I love him dearly and hope he sees it and speaks his truth someday on many things.

91

Chapter twenty-four

When it came to the nightmare blur of those two years, there were so many dark times. I was raising three babies and separating from their dad, and I found drinking more important than anything. I even lived in my car for a week with them because we were switching apartments and I had no one to turn to, not even him at the time. It never phased them. They thought we were just camping. When I started telling the truth more and trusting more people, I found my family in friends and support. It's crazy how, after all you've been through, you can find good in such tragedies, and I couldn't ask for more from them.

The kids' dad was on his own messed up journey with addiction and didn't prioritize anything except harassing me because I wouldn't be with him anymore, or because of his own selfishness. He never worked through his own trauma and abuse, so he didn't care about himself, let alone anyone else. That was the same path I was on for a while. I treated him badly and projected what we went through onto him. I lied, was violent, and manipulated when I drank. It was always his fault. I didn't do anything wrong because of what I'd been through, but I could never talk about it.

We had no fighting chance to be together when we didn't heal or love ourselves, let alone each other. We acted like our toxic parents, and everything that was shown to us as "love" and fake loyalty. We would fight on and off for each other and claim that was "love" in our own sick, twisted ways. We used the kids against each other. He was grieving his dad and so many things from his past. It was just absolutely too much for what we learned and what we'd been through from our own problems and abuse.

When I say during these times that it's what trauma recycles, that's not just me as a victim. There was a point where my kids were the only victims of this unhealed trauma and these cases. I yelled at them for everything because that was the only response I knew. I would get mad over the simplest things. I would drink and get mad if they disturbed it. When I was sober, it was like night and day. All my guilt came out, and I wanted to do everything with them, love on them, and be a good mom. But drinking was more important because I wouldn't stop.

I was hiding all this and wondering what happened. Why, why, why, why, why? That's all that ran through my head, and I didn't want to face it. I couldn't believe my family was trying to defend him and his family. It was insanity. My brothers went against me after everything, and there was so much resentment toward them and hatred toward my mom. I didn't realize it wasn't just about this case, but that my mom once again wasn't defending a child. And how many mothers do that? Absolutely sick.

I was afraid for my kids and always wondered, even after the interview, if they were too little to say something. The way I acted when I drank was erratic and selfish, but I was posting all over Facebook about how amazing I was as a mom. I wanted to be. I really did. I wanted to stop drinking, but I couldn't, and at the time, I didn't want to. I loved them the best I could, and sadly, my children will never say this, but it wasn't good enough or what they deserved, dealing with the demons from what happened that dreadful night in September and honestly, all my life.

I got the email that court was happening a week in March 2021. I knew it was no longer going to be delayed because they had me come to court to prepare me as one of the main witnesses. They asked me what happened, never adding anything or changing my statement, but just checking what I said, putting it down, and preparing me for the possibility that it might be scary, asking how I was feeling, and going over what I originally stated. Nothing changed; they didn't say or do anything to alter my statement, they just reviewed my true, original words.

Two days before court, I was drinking with a friend and wanted to meet another friend. I had my ex watch his kids while I went out. I ended up having to pee in a field, and some cops showed up and asked me what I was doing. I let my two dogs pee and poop, one had diarrhea and was a baby and I asked them if it was a crime to pee in a field. The cop responded that yes, ma'am, it was actually illegal to publicly urinate. I started acting on emotion, talking back, just being a straight brat. I had an unopened 12-pack of White Claws and an empty shaker in my cup holder.

He asked what was in the container. I said water. He said, "Don't play games." I said, "Don't talk to me like I'm stupid." He asked me to do a sobriety test. I don't know what made him think I was drunk maybe the public urination, maybe the belligerent attitude, maybe the yelling and insults? It was an absolute shock to me that they were accusing me of being drunk. That was my attitude at the time: everything was everyone else's fault, and how dare anyone stand up to me? I was "above the law," don't you know? That's complete sarcasm, just in case, because I know reading doesn't always convey tone.

They made me walk barefoot on rocks, which hurt my feet. They asked me to blow into a device, and I said absolutely not. Then they informed me that if I didn't, they would take me to the hospital to draw my blood. I said, "Go for it." I was in full "Britney badass" mode for a while, even yelling and telling them off. I told them I was a star witness in a high-profile pedophile case and to call the DA, saying I would get out of it. I know now that was nonsense. I know better now, and my point is that when you're in a raw, emotional state, your brain can come up with all kinds of irrational ideas. When you get better, accountability and common sense enter the picture.

They ended up looking up the case and realized I was telling the truth, but at that point, they didn't care, and I'm sure my attitude didn't help. I deserved it, they were just trying to do their jobs. My best friend came to pick up my dogs. She asked to speak to me, and the cops mentioned that if I acted up, they would close the window. The "Britney badass" in me melted away as soon as I heard her voice. I started crying so hard. She told me it was okay; they were going to take me to the hospital, and she would take the dogs to her house.

They took me to the hospital, and we waited and waited. I was being a smart ass the entire time, always quick to say something. I wasn't in the right state of mind and was angry more at myself than anything else for how I acted and for excusing my own actions. Cop 1 said, "Oh, they are going to get you when they take your blood." I responded, "Oh yeah, is this your first time?" Then Cop 2 said we were just waiting on a judge to approve the blood draw. I said, "Good luck with that." I kept going to the bathroom because my stomach was upset, but when I came out the second time, Cop 1 said, "You can pee all you want; it's not going to help." I said, "Well, no shit. They are taking my blood, and my stomach is upset. Is that okay with you?" He scoffed and asked what was in my shaker cup. He knew it wasn't water, and they were taking it to the lab to test. I started laughing. Unfortunately, because of how I grew up and the advantages I had, I knew the law and some of the tricks sometimes used, so I laughed some more. I told him if this was his first arrest, he got pissed and told Cop 2 he was going back out to call if needed. Cop 2 was on the laptop trying to call a judge and fill out paperwork.

As soon as the nurse pulled up with her cart next to me to take my blood, Cop 1 walked back in on the phone, saying, "Yes, sir. No, sir," and handed the phone to Cop 2. Cop 2 also said, "Yes, sir. No, sir," then replied, "No, we did not pull her over," and I just smiled. He finished with "Yes, sir. Understand, sir," and hung up. He handed the phone back to Cop 1, then Cop 2 came over, lifted me with my cuffs, and of course, I had to say, "Wait, what about my blood? Are they not going to take my blood?" I knew exactly what was happening and that the judge had said, "No, you can't get her blood." He was pissed and lifted me up aggressively. To be fair, given my attitude and comments, it was probably deserved, maybe worse, but that's how life works sometimes.

Even with the wrong mindset and attitude, you can win at life temporarily, but what you give to people and life comes back. I usually did the right thing, but the entitlement attitude was a cry for help, masked by the fear I had of everything else. They took me to jail. I called a friend, and she bailed me out. I paid her back and dealt with it. I had to tell the kids' dad where I was. He didn't ask many questions; he left it alone. Eventually, the charges were dropped. I got my official papers showing the charges were dropped one month after I got sober. It was a long process, but it was the hardest time of my life not because of the charge, since court was only a day away but because of everything leading up to it.

Chaptertwenty-five

First day in court. I got there early and waited all day in a small room. They kept saying I would be called next, over and over, and I was stuck in the room by myself for hours. At one point, you could hear into the hallway when everything was quiet, and people could speak. I was in full panic mode, with family saying things to me. My mom wondered why I was doing this, claiming that the child disgusted her. She was lying, and it hurt so badly. How could she keep doing this? How could she not protect an innocent child? Deep down, I understood that part of it was my hate for her, but it was still insane to hear.

My dad was my favorite. My best friend, the only person who always helped me, asked, "What do you have to gain from lying?" I told her they knew how much I loved my dad and our relationship. From the outside, what did I gain by doing this to him? Why would I stand against the only people I loved? Why would I go against my family? I saw him do it. I wasn't the only one; others saw him too. But the funny thing is, for believing in someone so strongly, she didn't show up once to court for him. She was there for support, nothing else not even to hear the evidence or cases. That made me so mad. At least be there to hear the truth or support the very man who put me through hell and told everyone I was a liar. She let everyone believe him instead of standing up for her child, or even herself, against something like this.

As I said before, an aunt once told me, "If this were your husband, you'd stand by him." I said, "I left my kids' father for less. Don't ever compare me to your disgusting family and upbringing. Protecting a child comes first. Against something like this, you don't sweep it under the rug or protect your own gain. You don't let someone abuse your child." As I said, there are many monsters in these cases, and that's why they are so hard.

I felt so crazy for so long. Even sitting in that room on the day of, I could not understand the fight or why it was so hard to put someone away. Even this long after everything, I was questioning myself at times. So many people made it seem like I was wrong for putting him away, for going to court to testify. They were outright mean, acting like defending a child was the most messed up thing I could do, that I should have been defending my dad after what he did. It is so sick and brutal what people have to go through and lose. At the time, it feels like a loss, but it absolutely is not. Like they say, surviving is strength. Doing the right thing can feel wrong and bring shame, which is why so many people have such a hard time coming forward to tell the truth. It is so damn sad and scary, especially when you have others making you feel like it is wrong, the very people you once called family.

When I was in the room, they came to talk to me and told me they would not be using me that day. They apologized for the weight of it all and said I would need to be there tomorrow at 8 a.m., and that I would be the first one going. After they said that, they went back into the courtroom and told me I could leave. The door was huge, and to the right were the double courtroom doors. As I was leaving, I heard the little one's voice. I heard them asking her questions, and it was his lawyer. He was not aggressive, just asking her questions about the reality of the relationship between the two of them. What made me sick was hearing the little one innocently say that he was her gampy, that she loved him, and that she had fun with him. Hearing her innocent, pure love as a child being used against her to try to say he did not do something he absolutely did, something so horrific to do to a child, made me feel sick.

I left with every single doubt and fear gone. I knew, like I felt before all the bashing, that I was doing the right thing. I knew I could speak for that little girl in ways she could not speak for herself. I always knew deep down that I was doing the right thing and protecting this child. I know what I saw and witnessed, I could replay it in my head like a video. Witnesses there saw the exact same thing.

That is the kind of thing enablers do, and why so many people get away with these kinds of crimes, because of manipulation and how we are taught to protect "family." It is so sick that it becomes this much of a fight, and that I was shamed so badly for defending a child. After that, I left with my head held high. I was beyond ready to protect this child, to protect her the way I should have been protected. It would not have mattered which child he hurt, the goal was to make sure he got what he deserved and to make sure he did not hurt another child again.

The next morning, I got ready and wore my lucky coat, which I still have to this day. I got ready, and my three best friends were there to support me, and it meant the world to me. I felt strong and ready, and I knew it was time to fight against the injustice silence we battle every damn day, through court or within ourselves, and for what happened to us and other children. The same injustice silence our families make us live with to keep our mouths shut, because that same man took care of us. I waited in the room, and then they came and called my name, and I was ready. I walked into that courtroom ready, ready to tell the truth and protect.

I walked in and glanced a mean look at his lawyer. My only thought was, how could you? How could you defend this against a child? I took the stand, was sworn in, and then I looked him straight in the eyes. Court began.

Epilogue

Revelations. Whoa, these. There is nothing like a huge, horrifying event in your life to bring out the truths in others. I am not going to lie to you, it was one of the hardest parts of what happened. At the time, as I was going through everything, I did not want to go through it alongside others. I wondered why they were telling me these things. I did not realize then that it was their own cries for help, spoken through their stories. When it first happened and I was navigating all my unknown emotions, I did not realize how important what they were telling me was, or how sharing their experiences and trauma would push me to take the stand and fight for all those who never got their words out and never got their justice.

To the friend whose mother did not defend you against her husband or boyfriend, I cannot say it enough. She should have protected you. You should have been her number one priority. I do not care what anyone else says. When it is you, her child, versus anything else, it should always be you.

To the friend who was groomed, and for those of you who do not understand that term, it is someone close in your life who made you believe their "love," and I cannot use quotation marks enough because it is not love. It is fake, manipulative affection that leads to inappropriate touching, "relationships," or financial situations that are excused because you were under 18. They pretended to be a father figure or another trusted adult in your life. That was and is wrong. They used your innocence and your naivety, and as blunt as this sounds, no father or mother figure would ever, ever lead you into abuse or sexual acts. Ever. Making it seem okay or trying to excuse it is why healing becomes so difficult.

To the friend who went to someone you trusted to share what happened to you, only for it to change your world, your thoughts, your feelings, and your mindset, and they asked you to sweep it under the rug or excuse it in many ways, I am sorry. You deserve that apology. You deserved protection. You deserved everything that was taken away from you that day, whether you are dealing with something that happened yesterday or damage from years ago. I am sorry. You deserve it all back. Nothing can change it, and nothing can fix it except yourself. It is not easy, and sometimes it can feel manageable, but not when someone you believe is on your team is holding you down. Not when you are a child and an adult you love and trust makes you feel this way, or even as an adult when someone still makes you feel wrong for doing the right thing.

That is the hardship and process of reading this and trying to understand what happened, how to move forward, and how to heal. This book and this experience are not a miracle, but they are part of the process I went through and what I experienced, in hopes that it helps in any way at all. This book was written to reveal my truths and trauma so others may feel inclined to share, speak up, and realize it is not just you, and you are not alone. Part two is all about life after. I hope you continue reading and joining me on my journey, because the silence of the tormented only seeks justice for the tormentor. #injusticesilence #hurtpeoplehurtorheal